In Heaven Everything is Fine

In Heaven Everything is Fine

a novel by
Jeffrey DeShell

FICTION COLLECTIVE TWO
Boulder•Normal•Brooklyn

Published by Fiction Collective Two. Additional support
given by the Publications Center of the University of
Colorado at Boulder, the New York State Council on the
Arts, Brooklyn College, and Teachers & Writers Collabora-
tive.

Address all inquiries to: Fiction Collective Two, c/o
English Department, Illinois State University, Normal,
Illinois 61761

DeShell, Jeffrey
  In Heaven Everything Is Fine

ISBN: 0-932511-39-2, $18.95
ISBN: 0-932511-40-6, $ 8.95

Manufactured in the United State Of America.

Distributed by the Talman Company

Grateful Acknowledgement is made for use of the following:

"A Song From Under the Floorboards," written by Barry Adamson, John McGeogh, Dave Tomlinson, Howard Devoto & John Doyle, (c) 1980 Virgin Music (Publishers) Ltd., lyrics reprinted by kind permission of Virgin Music (Publishers) Ltd,

"We're Desperate," X, Billy Zoom Music,

"Ha ha ha," Flipper, Subterranean Music,

"Jam On It," Newcleus, Wedot Music,

"The Days of Wine and Roses," 1982 Poison Brisket Music (BMI), Administered by Bug Music, All Rights Reserved/Used by permission,

"Love Will Tear Us Apart," Joy Division, Fractured Music,

"Watch Out For the Furniture," The Mutants

"Mutiny in Heaven," Nick Cave and the Bad Seeds, Dying Art Limited,

"What Use," Tuxedomoon, Pale Pachyderm Music,

"Doun De Road," written by Linton Kwesi Johnson (c) 1978 Virgin Music (Publishers) Ltd., lyrics reprinted by kind permission of Virgin Music (Publishers) Ltd,

"Heaven," (David Byrne, Jerry Harrison), (c) 1979 WB MUSIC CORP. All rights reserved. Used by permission,

"Sweet Jane," Lou Reed, (c) 1970 OAKFIELD AVENUE MUSIC LTD. , All rights controlled and administered by SCREEN GEMS-EMI MUSIC INC., All rights reserved. International Copyright Secured. Used by permission.

Portions of this novel have previously appeared in *Between C & D, The Moral Kiosk, Blatant Artifice* and *An Illuminated History of the Future*.

The author would also like to thank the Henfield Foundation for its generous support.

To Lisa Sheffield

3 am the characters assemble themselves in the flat Sweet Jane and I share Toulouse-Lautrec brings La Galoue and a couple of cases of champagne Sally comes in with Sweet Jane Frances Farmer Art and Sue Side arrive all talking at once Raoul shows up with a girl I've never seen before and a color tv the girl looks like she just stepped out of a Kirchner painting the tv's a beaut a Sony every time I see Raoul he brings me a color tv I don't know what this means Hey Raoul thanks for the tv want some champagne.

Sweet Jane and Sally go to the *Schizophrenic Bourgeoisie* to have a drink. Someone puts a quarter in the juke box Sweet Jane starts to dance all by herself. She starts out slow but as the tempo picks up she begins to move self-contained really beautiful. Next song Sally joins in the two of them heating up the men begin to notice. Another quarter hard fast beat the girls really get into the rhythm now the men crowd around to watch. One of the men throws a bill on the floor Sweet Jane undoes a button on her blouse. She moves really well gorgeous and teasing the men holler and whistle another dollar appears on the floor another button is unbuttoned everyone getting into the music now Sally takes the hint begins to tease lifts her t-shirt up and down the men whistle applaud hoot stamp their feet Sweet Jane undoes another button removes her blouse twirls it above her head then liberates her sweet breasts from her sweet bra the men love it an incredible pair of tits really nice. Another quarter in the juke box another dollar on the floor now it's Sally's turn she lifts the cotton up to her nipples slowly painfully slowly the men watch smile laugh applaud stick their hands into their pockets Sally lifts her shirt up to the tips hesitating then quickly over her head the men applaud cheer whistle Sally's nipples are erect. Sweet Jane already has the first button of her jeans undone grinding her hips a thin film of sweat now noticeable on her upper body the music shifts a slow raunchy number Sweet Jane unbuttons another button instantly commands everyone's attention even Sally's now another button Sweet Jane hooks her thumbs in her pants grinds her hips more bills and change appear along with a few suggestions she begins to pull her jeans down now visible brown panties the men going wild screaming laughing leering cajoling over her hips past her thighs the song changes she effortlessly steps out of her jeans. Sally stops dancing as if on cue begins to gather up the money Sweet Jane shows one cheek now the other now both keeps her hand over her crotch completely naked now except for that hand the men fondle themselves laugh drink holler and plead but as the song ends Sally and Sweet Jane run into the bathroom the men laugh slap each other on the back.

CORPSE SEX DAMAGE AWARD

Sacramento

The mother of a man whose body was stolen and sexually molested by an apprentice embalmer has been awarded $142,500 by a Sacramento Superior Court jury.

The jury deliberated more than seven hours before deciding Wednesday to award Marian Gonzales, 55, the $125,000 in compensatory damages and $17,500 in punitive damages.

Gonzales said during the trial that she suffered severe emotional damage after Greenlee, 23, stole a hearse containing the body of John Mercure, 33, on Dec. 17 of this year.

Greenlee subsequently admitted to police that she had sexual contact with Mercure's corpse and with up to 40 others while she worked at the mortuary.

A letter had been found with Mercure's body in which Greenlee described her first sexual contact with a corpse, and pleaded for help for her condition.

The letter said, "I've written this with what's left of my broken heart. If you read this, don't hate me. I was once like you. I laughed, I loved, but something went wrong. I'd give it all to know. But please remember me as I was, not as I am now."

I am angry I am ill and I'm as ugly as sin
My irritability keeps me alive and kicking
I know the meaning of life it doesn't help me a bit
I know beauty and I know a good thing when I see it
This is a song from under the floorboards
This is a song from where the wall is cracked
By force of habit
I am an insect
I have to confess I'm proud as hell of that fact

The woman Raoul brought over is sitting in the loveseat I pour a glass of champagne offer it to her Thank you You're welcome I don't believe I've seen you here before what's your name I've never been here before and I don't give my name out to strangers You must have a lot to hide I imagine everyone has a lot to hide very clever woman maybe a bit too clever if you know what I mean but she has the angles the lines the self-awareness the angst just right I will call her Kirchner's Woman.

Sally walking. Sally walking down a street Aspen Colorado. Sally intelligent beautiful unattached. Sally window-shopping American Express Mastercard Visa. Lunchtime five more shopping days till Christmas. Aspen Colorado a pleasant place for holidays snow and white everywhere. Sally tall graceful beautiful anonymous. Aspen Colorado full of beauty a town of perfection. Sally walking down a street Aspen Colorado Christmas shopping something wrong with this picture. Something wrong in the eyes of Carl Peterson age 26 of Denver Colorado. Who decided to die in Sally's arms.

Sally walking. Sally walking in the snow getting slightly hungry spinach salad maybe soup what to buy for Lise a man walks up to her says hello takes a pistol out of his pocket fires into his own mouth Sally jumps back the man begins to fall Sally tries to catch him too late he falls to the snow blood everywhere. Sally hears a scream puts the stranger's head in her lap begins to cry. Later Sally takes a hot bath fresh clothes hops in her car vague plans of California.

7:00 5 7 "Scruples" (Part 1) (1980) Lindsay Wagner, Barry Bostwick. The young wife of an elderly millionaire opens a Hollywood boutique and with the help of a handsome photographer and a New York fashion designer, soon turns it in to a huge success.
2 8 56 "Real People" Siamese Twins, a dog who eats with a fork, and a mother in Argentina who's had thirty-seven children.

It's hot. Maybe past ninety the asphalt streets melt in the sun. They sit naked in a bright room expensive furniture shiny hardwood floors. They have divided the room in half. They stare at each other listen to loud laughter in another room. The shock of recognition comes they suddenly see nothing but themselves in each other. The woman crosses over to him hands him a shiny black pistol. She leaves the room. He examines the pistol carefully thinks of how incredibly thirsty he is. Later they will make love on the shiny hardwood floors.

Art and Sue Side are sitting on the couch laughing and watching tv Toulouse is sitting watching everybody else Sweet Jane Sally Joe and La Galoue are dancing in the middle of the room Raoul is in another room talking on the phone Frances has had too much to drink is sitting on a chair in the corner staring at the floor I decide to try again Would you like to dance No but I would like another glass of champagne she holds her glass out to me jesus I think I need another cigarette.

Toulouse-Lautrec sits drinking in his studio waiting for La Galoue to arrive. The posters that Toulouse has printed have become great successes in a very short time, bringing wealth and critical acclaim to Lautrec, and instant fame to La Galoue (who is currently in negotiations with one of the major networks for a prime time variety special co-starring either Pat Sajak or John Davidson.)

Toulouse has been commissioned to print a series of six nude portraits of La Galoue for a very large sum of money. La Galoue was supposed to be at Lautrec's studio two hours ago, and he has no idea where she could be.

Toulouse-Lautrec is the city's favorite son right now; he even has had a drink named after him at that prestigious artists' watering hole, *The Banker*. Toulouse is confused by all this new-found fame and fortune; he's not sure exactly what it means. The money is nice, and he feels finally that he's getting the recognition he deserves, after all, he's worked very hard, so what could be wrong? Isn't he living every artist's dream? Why isn't he happy? Toulouse-Lautrec mixes himself another drink and waits.

EXCEPTIONAL

Tall, handsome, athletic, successful, affluent, Ivy League Senior corporation executive, 40, seeks an attractive female in her thirties for a lasting relationship. Interests include the arts, cultural events, gourmet food, fine wines, skiing, tennis, sailing, hiking. Box #5A.

Freaks was a thing I photographed a lot. It was one of the first things I photographed and it had a terrific kind of excitement for me. I just used to adore them. I still do adore some of them. I don't quite mean that they're my best friends but they make me feel a mixture of shame and awe. There's a quality of legend about freaks. Like a person in a fairy tale who stops you and demands you answer a riddle. Most people go through life dreading they'll have a traumatic experience. Freaks were born with trauma.

They've already passed their test in life. They're aristocrats.

Raoul comes into the room When I was in Mexico he begins I knew this Indian who believed the gods were pissed at him and the only way he could stay safe was to constantly surround himself with music he used to sit in the corner of the bar and sing softly to himself and he always had a couple of those five dollar transistor radios around him at all times for when he got tired of singing he wouldn't talk to you unless he trusted you real well I guess he thought you might be an assassin sent by the gods or something to knock him off if and when he did decide to trust you he would turn on all his radios and kind of sing to you you know tell his story in song so he offers me a ride home in his pickup one night got three or four radios turned up pretty loud and he starts singing to me how he used to work in this village making and fixing shoes until the son of one of the gods came down to get his shoes fixed and this son of a god fell in love with him and the father of the kid this god got real pissed you know figuring this guy had corrupted his young son or something and some of the other gods got mad too because this boy's really beautiful and they're jealous I mean here's this gorgeous son of a god in love with a fucking cobbler for chrissakes and this cobbler's got a wife and two kids I mean he don't even like boys so he's got five or six gods just ready to stomp him you know but this one goddess takes pity on him sleeps with him and tells him to get the hell away from his village and that as long as he can hear music he'll be safe that was about twenty years ago he hadn't seen his wife or kids in twenty years so anyway just as I was getting ready to split to come back here the old guy disappears can't find him anywhere they look and look finally find his truck in the bottom of a canyon nobody can figure out how the hell it got down there I mean there's no roads or nothing they find his truck alright but there's no sign of the old Indian but funny thing about the way they found the truck was by ear they heard it about a mile away there were at least a dozen radios surrounding the truck all going full blast.

Nerve gas works quickly, within minutes in a fatal dose. Victims first find their muscles beginning to spasm. They lose control of their bladder and bowels, and finally the muscles of the diaphragm become paralyzed. The victims suffocate.

There are no good antidotes to most chemical weapons, but atropine can reverse the effects of nerve gas. Unfortunately, atropine itself can be lethal if a soldier takes it when he has not gotten a dose of nerve agent.

We're desperate
Get used to it
We're desperate
Get used to it
We're desperate
Get used to it
We're desperate
Get used to it
It's kiss or kill

Kirchner's Woman lights a cigarette hands it to me Toulouse-Lautrec is sketching in his sketch book La Galoue dances over to him whispers something in his ear Lautrec whispers something in reply I'm not your fucking slave La Galoue screams you can't just order me around any time you feel like it I mean who in the fuck-ing hell do you think you are Lautrec says nothing just sits there quietly this infuriates La Galoue Answer me you son-of-a-bitch remember big shit artiste you have me to thank for all your success do you hear me me to thank without me you're nothing but a perverted midget the stories I could tell Lautrec turns red at this remark La Galoue spins on her heels and marches off to the kitchen Frances boozily shakes her head and for some reason follows La Galoue.

I'm sitting in *The Dirt Chute* trying to get quietly smashed I

15

want to feel I want to feel tragic hard-bitten cynical drunk Irish I sneer but I don't feel any of these things not even drunk. The way my life's been going lately I should feel something sad depressed something I mean I have the right but I just shrug it off no highs or lows just one continuous shrug.

I am not having a good time. This is the place where fifteen year old boys come fresh off the bus. Low ceiling, smell of sweat, amyl nitrate and vaseline. Three seats down a fellow giving a guy a hand job under the bar. The guy beside me drinking a frozen strawberry daiquiri. Just another shrug. The silence beyond the scream. Level out shrug it off be cool. It's what you know that makes you go it's what you learn that makes you squirm. The beat indeed goes on. This is my cool funk hipster persona how do you like. It is so hip because all of us cool funk hipsters start the next sentence with the last word of the. Previous research has shown that language determines thought or is it the other way. Around here language seems to be the only gesture left that one can even partially. Understand this everyone's life a series of one misunderstood gesture after. Another brandy please I'm not feeling that clever the boy next to me sad lonely puts a Marlene Dietrich record on the juke box because when one is sad and lonely this is the appropriate music to put on the juke box it's expected even though the music's the thing and nobody cares who played it or why just another wasted gesture. The inevitability of cliché.

Sitting here shrugging it off I'm here because the drinks are cheap. Also, I like the smell of vaseline.

TOP ITEM SHOPLIFTED IN DRUGSTORES:
  Preparation H.
NUMBER OF TIMES CAUGHT:
  One in 49 attempts.
NUMBER OF TIMES PROSECUTED:
  One in 98.
AVERAGE THEFT:
  $96 value.

AVERAGE FREQUENCY OF THEFT:
   Daily, 13.2%; weekly, 14.2%; monthly, 30.4%.
AVERAGE THEFT, BY TYPE OF STORE:
   Department store, $100; convenience store, $2.

Before you awake I go downstairs buy croissants strawberries and a paper I come back up you've made coffee kiss me good morning the light soft hazy Billie Holliday on the radio we dance then lie down eat the strawberries off of each other's bodies I cradle you in my arms you begin to cry it's 1954.

Frances and La Galoue return Frances sprawls on the couch next to Sue and Art La Galoue dances with Raoul Kirchner's Woman walks over stands behind the couch watches television I hear Art ask Frances what her favorite city is Baltimore she says I'm looking at Kirchner's Woman's ass wonder why Baltimore but nobody asks.

Bad night for Sally. Emergency room duty 5:30 am a self-abortion death due to massive internal hemorrhaging the girl bled to death in her own womb. Blood everywhere the floor slick the doctor's coat soaked red on white tile red on white cotton red on white. Sally feels something awful stir in her own belly a fucking butcher knife she used a fucking butcher knife hysteria very near the surface. Sally a nurse Sally a woman Sally trying to fill out the report can't read. Black marks on white paper. No sense. Sally trying hard to comprehend trying hard to force meaning into the markings no use no sense. The markings mean nothing. Not another language no language. Language does not exist. Red on white.

POET & CRITIC Iowa State University Press, David Cummings, English Dept., ISU, 203 Ross Hall, Ames IA 50011. Poetry, articles, art, interviews, satire, criticism, reviews. "Selected contributors comment on each other's work."

So often, in the course of my life, reality had disappointed me because at that instant when my senses perceived it my imagination, which was the only organ that I possessed for the enjoyment of beauty, could not apply itself to it, in virtue of that ineluctable law which ordains that we can only imagine what is absent.

Toulouse-Lautrec finishes his sketch hands it to Sweet Jane kisses her hand then silently sits back down Sweet Jane smiles acts pleased passes the drawing around it's a sketch of Sweet Jane in a white evening gown La Galoue looks a bit put-off whispers something to Sweet Jane who stares coldly back at her confrontation imminent Sally takes Sweet Jane by the hand leads her into the bathroom La Galoue starts to dance alone in the middle of the room is soon joined by Joe and Raoul my glass is completely empty I stare into it Kirchner's Woman begins to laugh.

Five Questions People Often Ask Joe:
   1) Are you okay?
   2) Are you in a band?
   3) Will you excuse me?
   4) Do you work here?
   5) Do you know what time it is?
Five Questions People Never Ask Joe:
   1) Can I stay for breakfast?
   2) Will you do that to me all night?
   3) Would you like some more drugs?
   4) Can I see you again?
   5) Where have you been all my life?

DEAR ABBY: I am an Illinois state senator. Regardless of how anyone else feels about homosexuality, it galls me that sexual deviates are called "gays."

The word "gay" means joyous, merry, happy and cheerful, as opposed to gloomy, melancholy, dejected or miserable. Therefore, to describe homosexuality as "gay" is a perversion in itself and I respectfully request you discontinue the use of the word in that context.

Instead of the word "gay", the word "queer" would be more appropriate. "Queer" means to deviate from the normal or expected.

In my opinion, the truly "gay" people of the world are heterosexuals who have relations with persons of the opposite sex.

Won't you join me in an effort to retrieve the word "gay" from ignominy? And if the word "queer" is unacceptable to describe deviates, then confine their definition to "homosexuals." - NAME WITHHELD ON REQUEST.

Art should never try to be popular; the public should try to make itself artistic.

The music stops Sally and Sweet Jane return from the kitchen Raoul switches off the tv everyone sits around the table in silence oh no I can feel it something stupid is about to happen a Very Important Discussion perhaps I start to get up Toulouse speaks No No please sit down I have something very important to discuss with you as you know I how do you say 'caught' your act at the *Maroon Lagoon* the other night your routine was most amusing indeed you are a very funny fellow but tell me my dear man what did you mean when you said and I quote Art is a garden nothing more nothing less one takes some dirt a few pepper seeds some tomato seeds cucumber seeds a few strawberry seeds seeds of corn squash and wild zucchini seeds of leek watercress and watermelon bulbs of two varieties of potato sticks them all in the dirt adds a little shit keeps out the weeds and insects and *viola* something beautiful arises out of the ground where there was once only wet shit and furthermore the more shit one puts on this creation the more beautiful it seems to grow now that I've got you here my friend do you really think all art is just shit.

Name: Sue Side
Age: 21
Height: 5'9"
Weight: 109 lbs.
Hair: Black
Eyes: Blue
Favorite Authors: Norman Mailer, Jay McIrnerny, Bret Easton Ellis, Tom Wolfe.
Favorite Artists: Norman Rockwell (really!), Andy Warhol, David Hockney.
Favorite Music: Sinatra, Talking Heads, Rap.
Favorite Things to Do;   Walk on the beach, eat at a fancy restaurant, go dancing with my friends, buy new clothes, make love out of doors.
Things Desired in a Man: Muscular, athletic, well-built and rich. Fun-loving men are great, but ya gotta have money to have a good time.

Indiana's drivers received stickers instead of license plates this year. But some Hoosiers have been licking the tags thinking they work like stamps. They don't. And the stickers have had to be removed from the tongues of the quick-lickers at the hospital.

4:00 he turns on the tv and hears sirens. The sirens he hears on tv echo the sirens he hears outside. He puts his hand over his ears that doesn't help the sirens have him surrounded crescendoing decrescendoing just when you've gotten it small enough to deal with (never stopping it but at least slowing it down) along comes something else he begins to scream. The sirens stop but there's a knock at the door.

Actually I think Art's kind of a jerk takes himself much too seriously I say Oh yeah well fuck you says Sue Are you speaking metaphorically asks Toulouse You really are an asshole says Art

Look who's calling the kettle black says Raoul the only difference between performance art and punk rock is that at least punk rock has music Kirchner's Woman laughs again Frances belches loudly rises quickly makes it to the bathroom throws up Sally puts a record on Sweet Jane Sally and Raoul start to dance.

Drugs. A necessary element to many adventures including discovering the true meaning of the phone cord and sleeping with repellent strangers.

Smack, scag, junk, horse, H, stuff, stash, snow, sugar, garbage, rubbish, Mexican Brown, China White, Malaysian Yellow, Moroccan Silver, Idaho red, opium, hope, poppy juice, dream honey, blue steel, Lenny Bruce, black gold, Texas tea, now first thing you know ole Jed's a millionaire. . . .

Yes, our heroine was on heroin, Sweet Jane is an ex-junkie, or in the process of becoming one actually; she now goes to the methadone clinic twice a week.

Sweet Jane used to be Plain Jane, a rather awkward girl who was born and raised in Omaha. She was ugly before ugliness was considered hip, she was homely before her time. And I do mean homely!

Six foot two one hundred three pounds. Ratty black hair, oozing pimples, absolutely no breasts, and spaghetti-like legs attached directly to her torso without the aid of an ass. The girl was so ugly, when she was born the doctor took one look at her and slapped her mother. She was so ugly that she had bruises all over her body from people touching her with ten foot poles.

So one bright sunny day in a clean upstairs apartment someone offered her a needle. She had nothing to lose, junkies were the only people who talked to her anyway, so why not and as easy as pie she had her first taste.

She liked it, liked it a lot. Soon she wanted to be constantly nodding, constantly in another consciousness. She liked the clarity that the drug and the need for the drug gave her. She liked having the entire universe reduced to one thing.

The junk began to have strange effects on her body. Her skin cleared up and she found an appetite and began to put on weight in all the 'right' places.

One day, after a couple of months of constant nodding, she happened to see her reflection in a mirror at Woolworths. The image shocked her, she was beautiful beyond recognition. She saw a gorgeous girl of nineteen, with shiny black hair, lean aristocratic features, and a well-shaped voluptuous body. She couldn't believe her eyes.

Soon she thought that she began to get a little too chubby, so she started going to the methadone clinic twice a week. Methadone keeps her looking just right.

Sweet Jane met Sally at the clinic, where Sally sometimes works as a nurse. They have become best friends.

Sweet Jane hasn't slept with anybody since she became beautiful.

COPS UNCOVER AMPUTEE HOAX

Tokyo (AP) - The long arm of the law has caught up with 12 residents of a western Japanese village who cut off some of their fingers to obtain insurance money.

Police in Kawasaki Town on the island of Kyusho said as many as 70 people in the area had dismembered themselves to qualify for compensation. In addition to the 12 amputees arrested, police said they detained six people who masterminded the operation, including one who received about $400 per person for cutting off the fingers of at least four people.

Isn't life a blast
It's just like living in the past
And we go downtown to do our shopping
But we live in suburbia
And I say
Ha Ha Ha Ha Ha Ha Ha Ha

Ho Ho Ho Ho Ho Ho Ho Ho
He He He He He He He He
Ha Ha Ha Ha Ha Ha Ha Ha

I ask Kirchner's Woman why she's laughing she says I just think it's amazing the level of misunderstanding going on here don't you I mean all of the routines and objects which we attach special significance to nobody else has the faintest clue as to what they mean or how important they are to us do you understand Yeah kind of like when Frances said Baltimore and nobody even asked why Exactly but it can be even more frustrating to have your objects misunderstood after all words are just words But what if your whole life was misunderstood she looked at me and started to laugh again.

ART
by Art
Fuck ART, let's dance
Fuck dance, let's Art
Lets' dance and fuck, the ultimate ART
My performance is like a sexual experience, both for me (the performer)
and for you (not the performer)
Don't just sit there on your hands
Sit on my hands
Dance on my hands
Fuck on my hands
Put flaming coals under my fingernails
Do ANYTHING!
But do ART
Any body can ya know
Do ART
do Art

ART is nothing more than. . . .
ART is nothing less than. . . .
ART is nothing
Art is nothing
I am nothing
You are less (more) than nothing
You can be a happy nothing
Watch
DO!!!
You MUST choose:

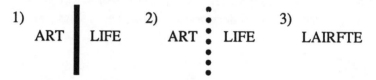

1)
    ART   LIFE   2)   ART : LIFE   3)   LAIRFTE

Society is a function of ART
Everything you have ever read or heard is ART
ART is:
1) Guerilla warfare
2) Really good *safe* sex
3) A rectal thermometer
4) Ice cream
5) Genocide
6) Pornographic books
7) Setting fire to Burger King
8) Stealing used clothes
9) Attempting suicide (and failing)
10) My performance, July 17, La Gallerie Vaché, 1220 21st St.

ART is not:
1) Painting of any kind
2) Posters or prints of any kind
3) Sculptures of any kind

4) Writings of any kind except pornography
5) Architecture of any kind
6) Food of any kind
7) Collage of any kind
8) Film of any kind including video
9) Anything of any kind
10) My performance, July 17, La Gallerie Vaché, 1220 21st St.

I spend an entire day mending fences, and do you know what they bring me? Light beer. Didja ever taste light beer?
It's Coors Light. Try it.
Hmmm. Not bad. Not bad at all.

Oh, plenty of hope, an infinite amount of hope - but not for us.

She lights another cigarette hands it to me I ask what do you think is the single most misunderstood thing about you That's a good question a very good question she says nothing for a while I would have to say my gender Your gender Yeah my gender That's not really a thing is it I think so I think the most misunderstood thing about me is my gender Why Well some people think I'm a cunt So what some people think I'm a real prick What does that mean Nothing it was just a joke Anyway people tend to treat me more as something to fuck instead of a person they don't treat me as someone with ideas and feelings they treat me just as something to put their dick into even you just now you were staring at my ass you want to fuck me the reason you're being so nice to me is because you want to fuck me you do want to fuck me don't you Jesus I don't know Just admit it just admit that you want to fuck me Okay I want to fuck you That's okay I'm not angry there's nothing wrong with wanting to fuck someone but do you see what I mean No not really.

DANNY AND THE DERRIDEANS - Angels On All Fours
Side A   Plato's Pharmacy

Glas
Van Gogh's Shoes (Sometimes I Feel So Unconcealed)
Nothing Outside of the Text
Post Cards
Side B Imagination is Freedom
Violence and Metaphysics
Dangerous Supplement
So Tired of Being Alone
DANNY AND THE DERRIDEANS
Sweet Jane - Guitar, Vocals
Sue Side - Bass, Vocals
Dorra Jarr - Guitar, Keyboards, Tape Loops, Vocals
Curtis Interruptus - Percussion, Tympanum
Neal Expressionism - Electronics, Vocals
   All songs by DANNY AND THE DERRIDEANS except "So Tired of Being Alone" by Al Green. Lyrics reprinted by permission. Wicked Puppy Music ASCAP. Recorded in San Francisco at Dry Hole Studios. Engineered and produced by DANNY AND THE DERRIDEANS. Another Acid Rain Artist. Thanks to Frances Farmer. Artwork by Lautrec.

WHAT'S MODERN: ATTITUDE
   Either intense anxiety or committed frivolity. Anything less than the first betrays lack of depth, anything less than the second betrays lack of grace.

POEM
Richard Pryor caught on fire
I was trotting along and suddenly
it started raining
and you said it was motherfucking hailing
but motherfucking hailing hits you on the head
hard so it was really snowing and
raining and I was in such a hurry
to meet you but the traffic
was acting exactly like the sky

and suddenly I see a headline
RICHARD PRYOR CAUGHT ON FIRE!
there is no snow in Hollywood
there is no rain in California
I have been to lots of parties
and acted perfectly disgraceful
but I never actually caught on fire
oh Richard Pryor we love you chill out

Why do men want to fuck me I don't know jesus christ Why
do you want to fuck me Is this a test No but answer anyway What
if I don't answer does that mean we'll never fuck Just answer the
question I don't know I guess I find you attractive What does that
mean I don't know let's change the subject Come on be more
specific why do you want to fuck me I 'd really like to know Well
I can't speak for all men but I think you have a pretty face and a
nice ass and Do you want to fuck every women with a pretty face
and a nice ass No you didn't let me finish I don't think you have
AIDs and I think you're intelligent I find intelligence a real turn-
on Why I don't know who wants to fuck somebody stupid I mean
what's the point You know something I don't think you're all that
different from other men Do you know something I don't think
you're that much smarter than other women.

Match Frances' action with the headlines:
    A) DEATH COUNT CLIMBS IN IRAQ
    B) FRANCE STUNNED BY CHILDREN'S DEATH
    C) PRESIDENT OK'S HUGE DEFENSE BUDGET
    D) SEX SCANDAL ROCKS CABINET
    E) ACCOMPLICE LEADS POLICE TO MASS GRAVE
    1) Bought a new VCR
    2) Spray painted FUCK YOU on the Bank of America
       building
    3) Got drunk and smashed up her car

4) Bought a Tiffany necklace
5) Gave Sweet Jane $2000 to help record the album

One of these days Alice, one of these days - BAM, ZOOM, to the moon Alice, TO THE MOON!

What did the polack do with his first fifty cent piece?
He married her.
What's red and has seven dents?
Snow White's cherry.
What do you call a truckload of vibrators?
Toys for twats.
Why couldn't the little greek boy leave home?
He couldn't leave his brother's behind.
What does an elephant use for a vibrator?
An epileptic.
And remember, you can't stop masturbating gradually, you've got to do it cold jerky.

Frances emerges from the bathroom says I'm ready to go will someone please call me a cab Okay you're a cab says Art You're real fucking funny says Frances I'll call a cab for you says Sweet Jane Art walks up to Kirchner's Woman and me So are you two going to fuck or just talk about it all night I wish someone would fuck you to shut you up says Raoul It's people like you who give faggots a bad name says Art Yeah really says Sue Okay everybody calm down now says Sally Who the fuck do you think you are says Art Florence Fucking Nightingale C'mon Art calm down you're making a scene says Sweet Jane Oh heaven forbid that I should cause a disturbance in your home where I merely a guest O I humbly beg your pardon if I have annoyed you true bohemians in any way shape or form O you charter members of the avant-garde O you true artists of real life rest assured that I will never darken your doorway again farewell forever c'mon Sue let's get the fuck outta here.

10 am no sleep Joe hears the doorbell ring. He calmly drains his glass and just as calmly pours himself another. All thought drowned out by the bell's reverberation. He stares at the bottom of his glass. The chime repeats penetrating deeply into his brain. He walks quietly to the front door and waits. He can hear something rustling on the other side. He wants to know who or what is out there. He doesn't move, listens and waits. The bell rings a third time he opens the door slowly. "Hello sir my name is Bobby and I'm with the Neighborhood Youth League and I'm selling candy to earn my way to camp I've got chocolate-covered cherries almond nougat caramels peanut brittle and salt water taffy only two dollars a box please sir can you help me?"

Joe recoils, then smiles. "Sure kid justa second." He shuffles back into the house and finds his wallet on the table. He picks up a bill without looking it's a twenty.

"I'll take two boxes of those cherries there, a couple of the nougat, and three of the peanut brittle," he hands him the bill, "and give me my change in taffy, okay kid."

SAFE
Dry Kissing
Oral Sex with a Condom
Masturbation on Healthy Skin
External Watersports
Touching
Fantasy
POSSIBLY SAFE
Protected Vaginal Intercourse
Protected Anal intercourse
RISKY
Wet Kissing
Oral Sex without a Condom
Masturbation on Open/Broken Skin
Oral Sex on a Woman

Amphetamines (speed)
Amyl Nitrite (poppers)
Alcohol
Marijuana
DANGEROUS
Unprotected Vaginal Intercourse
Unprotected Anal Intercourse
Internal Watersports
Intravenous Drugs
Sharing a Needle
Fisting
Rimming

Love, love will tear us apart, again.
Yes love, love will tear it apart, again.

The party disintegrates Kirchner's Woman asks me What do you think is the single most futile gesture I'm tired of this interrogation Masturbation I say That's interesting you could be right but what about sex in general I mean sleeping with somebody of the opposite gender seems so futile it doesn't take into account the fundamental differences between men and women I mean we're two completely different species with completely different thought processes but on the other hand homosex seems so boring and useless where's the discovery where's the strangeness it doesn't seem worth it well anyway I have to go here's my address I'll cook you dinner Wednesday night seven o'clock Speaking of sex why don't you spend the night with me tonight Actually it did cross my mind but I don't really appreciate your taste in music.

2:30 am Raoul calls Sweet Jane no answer he hangs up after twelve rings. He dials another number at random.
"Hello? Who is this?"
"Auschwitz, Dachau, Birkenau, Treblinka, Hiroshima, Kampuchia, Beirut, Gaza . . . ."

"Hello? Who is this?"

"The nazis used to cut sections out of the flesh of women prisoners and later sew it back in just to make them less attractive. Some of the experiments involved the attempted insemination of female prisoners with monkey sperm."

CLICK

"A doctor in the United States perfected an easy and relatively quick method of lobotomy where an ice pick-like instrument was inserted through the eye-socket into the brain. This severed several neural passages and made the patient more docile and easy to manage. This permanent personality change was practiced throughout the United States until the early 60's. . . ."

A personal finance seminar will be held at 7 pm Sunday through Wednesday at First Assembly of God Church, 25th and Junction Streets. The seminar, called "God's Principles for Financial Freedom" will be conducted by the Reverend Dave Weeks and is open to the public. The seminar is based on the belief that the Bible contains very specific directions for money management, and that it's no sin to be rich.

Who in Love's name dares to speak of Hell?

I arrive late to a party given by a painter to honor the opening of another painter's show I see Raoul talking to Sweet Jane and Sally I find a glass of wine and walk over to them Has Kirchner's Woman left yet Sweet Jane asks me I didn't know she was leaving I reply Sally and Sweet Jane look at each other Where is she going I demand Sally hesitates then says New York I think she might have already left I didn't know she was leaving I repeat as if knowledge could make any difference.

Raoul and Sweet Jane are talking in the bathroom. Both are quite drunk.

"Do you believe in God, Raoul?"

"I want more than anything else to believe in God. But look around you, and you see that such belief is impossible. I do, however, believe in angels. The existence of pain and the existence of angels are the only two things I am certain of. Angels who appear from nowhere, heavily made up in stiletto heels. Angels sitting alone, drinking, trying to fog that flame of shameful, pure desire. Angels who never touch the ground, but who walk always a few inches above, and who shy away from that light green incandescent glow of hysterical indifference. Angels who arrive early and stay late, all the while with their eyes fixed on the door, as if their executioner savior was but a few steps behind, and who leave not in a flurry of coats, toasts and smiles, but who disappear silently, like the dot fading out on the television screen. Angels who know compassion because they have sat all night at some dirty window, staring at the cracked streetlight, their foreheads pressed against the frozen glass. Angels who can hear the ambiguous silence of an empty bed, mocking and inviting them, driving them onto the linoleum indecision of a bright kitchen floor. Angels who know death each moment they are happy, and who know that true terror lies in realized kisses. Angels who never make good lovers because they are always far too grateful. Angels whose wings cannot stand the scrutiny of sunlight or sobriety. Angels who reduce everything to image and therefore feel nothing but regret. Angels made visible by their silver breath in the darkened playground. Angels who comprehend the equations of affection. Angels whose lipstick resembles blood on snow. Angels who mold truth like soft clay in order to fashion tools for survival. Angels who seek out those who cannot walk, for companionship, not wisdom. Angels who yearn for tenderness with every single cell but feel the nausea of disgust when dreams come true. Angels who. . . . "

"You're getting rather hysterical, Raoul."

"Of course I am. There seems to be only two types of people today, those who are hysterical and those who are plastic. I prefer hysteria myself, it proves that one is alive."

"But isn't hysteria just another form of plasticity? And vice-versa? It's easy to be numb, but it's just as easy to be crazy. I find both extremes extremely dull."

"Men have to learn to be kind, while women have to learn to be cruel. That is why all men who start out loving women end up hating them."

"I don't think I was being cruel, but I'd rather be cruel than wrong."

Raoul sighed. "One can be certain one is being kind, yet one can never be certain one is correct. Some people have many opportunities to become angels, yet they refuse. Others never have the opportunity at all."

"But how can angels exist without God?"

"God cannot exist without angels, but angels can exist without God. Look around you."

"What about good and evil?"

"Evil is indifference."

"And good?"

"The existence of a thing does not imply its opposite. Evil is silence, that is all."

Coping With Loss? Separation, divorce, death, unemployment, miscarriage, abortion, material loss, other - mixed adult group now forming! Patrick J. Ahern, C.S.W., A.C.S.W.. Diane L. Carter, M.S. 263-0031 (downtown location).

Art students tend to see themselves as exceptions to the social rule: they don't have to conform, they can avoid as one said to me, "the restraints and responsibilities of the 9 to 5 world." They see themselves as the superior amoral minority in the moral majority, the free spirits among the inferior slaves. They aspire to the tired Nietzschean myth of elitist non-conformity - of avoiding a fate worse than death, the living death of everyday life; at the same time, they are unconsciously - as well as not so unconsciously, conformist. Their different drummer marches a well-traveled route to a familiar tourist attraction.

They want success, on their own unique terms - as everyone does. They want the rewards, tangible and intangible. As one wrote, they want "Money, glamour/fame, parties/openings" - in that order; that is, from the commonplace to the exclusive. They have no more sense of self than other people concerned to "make their mark."

I've never seen so many haircuts in my entire life says Raoul I've never seen so many bad haircuts says Sweet Jane Why is Kirchner's Woman going back to New York I ask I think she's going back to try to patch things up with her husband she was married once you know to a well-known playwright No I didn't know that Yeah when they separated he poked tiny holes in her diaphragm with a pin That's brilliant says Raoul fucking brilliant

When is she leaving I ask I think she's supposed to leave real soon says Sally I thought she already left says Sweet Jane I need another drink.

"Oh Toulouse, for heaven's sake, don't be such a baby about it, it happens to everyone. It really is no big deal. You're just nervous or something, or you've had too much to drink. I like the kissing and the other stuff the best anyway. Don't worry, *mon petit homme.* C'mon, don't just sit there and sulk, the light's still good and we can still get some work done. C'mon sweetheart, let's go, I'll give you my absolutely prettiest face. Please Henri, please."

POOR FARM TRANSFORMED INTO ELEGANT INN
Salida - The people who once lived here were called inmates, not guests. Many lived here in shame. The Poor Farm was the only place left for those who had nowhere else to go.

It would be unimaginable to the first occupants that this same building designed in 1892 to house the lame, the blind and the destitute could be transformed into a vacation spot. Yet today, in the shadows of the Collegiate Range to one side and the Sangre De Christo mountains on the other, this once dingy institution has become an elegant bed and breakfast inn savored by those with taste for graceful living, quiet beauty, fine dining and lovely antiques.

You can't lug the corpse of your father all over the place.

I go to get a drink and I run into Sue side and Art arm in arm giggling and drinking heavily How are you Art asks I just love parties Sue Side says I just loooooove watching all the people Yeah says Art I think I saw Jean-Michel here he hates Michael's work but he loves Roberto's parties hey a bunch of us are going over to Eva's tonight she just got that grant so she's buying some drugs why don't you come along I don't think so That girl you were talking to the other night's going to be there she's good friends with Eva Oh yeah maybe I will go Look some rappers says Sue Well see ya says Art Yeah see ya says Sue Side.

DANNY AND THE DERRIDEANS

I don't know what it was, but something made me think twice about reviewing a show by a band named for a contemporary French philospher. I mean, what if this started some sort of trend - would the *Kans and the Kants, Descartes and Dehorse,* and the *Young Hegelians* be far behind? I'm not quite sure the world is ready for *Husserl's Greatest Hits.*

Quite frankly, I didn't know what to expect. Comparisons ranging from the old *Joy Division* to *Run DMC* to *Throbbing Gristle* have been in the air at cocktail parties, staff meetings, gallery openings and taco stands for the past couple of weeks. At the Green Carnation the other night I ran into somebody who, get this, almost actually heard them! He described them as a sort of *Laurie Anderson* on speed. No, he didn't know who *Derrida* was, but he did have some books at his place, and he was getting bored with this scene, so why didn't we go back to his loft for some heavy reading . . . .Well, I thanked him politely and went on my way. Maybe I've been in LA too long, but I've developed a deep mistrust of just about everything, especially things that everyone likes but no one's seen or heard. I like to make my cynical little post-technological mind up for myself. And maybe I'm tired of all these so-called "intellect" bands trying to mix half-formed esoteric ideologies (which they don't understand anyway) with rock-n-roll, because usually the ideas are incoherent and the music sucks. And maybe I think that any band from San Fran is probably composed of boring little wankers from the Art Institute who all have friends dying of AIDS and gobs of money. Besides, I hadn't seen a video, and if it ain't good enough for LATV, then it ain't good enough for *moi.*

So it was with some trepidation that I joined the rather stylish crowd at Che's the other night. It seemed like everybody was there, from Irvine Comparative Literature Professor *Andrzej Warminski* to *Black Flag's Henry Rollins*. *Bill Burroughs* was there, drinking brandy and milk, along with the California art world's latest *enfant terrible, Toulouse-Lautrec*. The place was absolutely swamped with celebs, and famous people are my favorite animals, so I thought that maybe this wouldn't be such a bad evening after all. I'd have a few drinks, listen to what hopefully would be a tolerable show, and then try to corner *Burroughs* or *Lautrec* for an interview. *Jonathan Culler* asked me to sit at his table, and as I took my seat, the lights dimmed.

The band was quite simply fantastic. Imagine *Magazine* with Raskolinikov himself singing lead, or *Tuxedomoon* backing *Baudelaire*. Imagine a hybrid of *Heidegger* and *James Brown,* of *Tel Quel* and *Public Enemy*, of the *Quartier Latin* and *Motown*. I never knew radical philosophy could be so much fun.

If structuralism doesn't fight in the streets, post-structuralism sure does dance in them. Even *Bill Burroughs* got up and danced with *Tina Turner,* and let me tell you for a fact that he can still shake his money-maker. If I were only a couple of years older...(Watch it, ED.) The band roared through their post-everything funk at a furious pace. The fast songs, "Nothing, Nothing, Nothing Outside of the Text," "Imagination is Freedom," and "Plato's Pharmacy" blew the roof off the place, while the slower, razor sharp versions of "Play," "Van Gogh's Shoes (Sometimes I Feel So Unconcealed)" and "Glas," were honed to a stiletto point. The encore, a new piece entitled "Violence and Metaphysics" brought tears to my eyes as I swayed to the hypnotic beat of Sue Side's bass and Curtis Interruptus' syncopated snare, juxtaposed against Dorra Jarr's soaring synthesizers and Neal Expressionism's found sounds and electronic noises. And above all this, Sweet Jane sang, screamed, wailed and whispered. It was one moment this writer will never forget.

After the show, at a party given by *Greil Marcus* for the band, I did mange to record an impromptu interview with all five band members, which will be published in the next issue. For now, all

37

I can say is that if you ever get a chance to see this band, drop EVERYTHING! and go! And to paraphrase *Derrida* himself, Play, Play, Play!

IN MY OPINION
A Public Service of Channel 2

In my opinion, something should be done to stop those adults from making all of those atomic bombs. Instead of making all those bombs which would kill everything on earth, people should think about ways to stop hunger, pollution and war.

These bombs are no good. I don't hate anybody, not even the Russians. The Russians are not bad people, we should not want to kill all of the Russians. I don't know any Russians but if I saw one I would want to talk with him, play with him and stuff, I would not want to kill him.

In school we learned that both America and Russia have enough atom bombs to kill everything many times over. I'm just a kid, but that does not even sound right to me. My daddy says I don't understand these things, and he's right. Why do we need enough bombs to kill people more than once?

And what about me and my friend's futures? I heard some kids say why not take drugs and stuff and why do good in school because we're all just going to get blowed up anyway. This is a kid's world just as much as a grown-up's world, and grown-ups don't have any right to get everyone blowed up. So please don't make no more bombs, and please don't kill no more. I'm Jimmy Machlis, and that's my opinion.

It's mostly love that makes you look at fine ankles and then break them. The ankle is where the moving power of the leg tapers to an exquisite stem of bone. Sadly, the foot comes next, anchoring wonderful creatures to the dirt. Deer, wading birds, and the best people all have fine ankles. It's good to crack their supports so they'll fall down in a lovely curl. Then you'll care for them so they will be free from all crassness and struggle. You'll watch the shattered ankles heal and meanwhile, the creatures will live in a state of grace and suspended animation.

Jesus you look down Sweet Jane says are you okay No I'm not okay I'm not okay god damn it I turn to Raoul what does one do when all the mechanisms for disgust have broken down Raoul laughs Don't get maudlin my boy you're far too young But I'm tired of paying for everything with blood Raoul laughs again Suffering is the only thing we don't have to pay for suffering is its own reward now cheer up okay for chrissakes cheer up.

Perpetual self-consciousness breeding paralysis I'm sitting with Sweet Jane and Sally in Frances Farmer's apartment trying to talk Frances out of suicide no in reality nothing as dramatic as that. Actually we're just sitting and speeding watching cable tv THE ROLLING STONES ISRAELI TROOPS TAMPAX TED KOPPEL THE BALTIMORE ORIOLES DEMOCRATIC NATIONAL CONVENTION JAZZERCISE ON GOLDEN POND HIGHLY CONTROVERSIAL ABORTION RULING CENTRAL AMERICA IT'S A SONY CHRYSLER BOB HOPE SPECIAL PARTLY CLOUDY WITH A CHANCE OF RAIN THE SHOOTIST MARY TYLER MOORE BACH'S GREAT-EST PIANO CONCERTOS SOLID OAK DINETTE SET A FILIBUSTER IN THE SENATE TODAY HONEY I'M HOME IN LIBYA LAST NIGHT WALL STREET JOURNAL BAR-FLY HOTLIPS HAVE YOU SEEN FRANK DAN RATHER AAAAAAAAAAAAAWESOME OUR CHANNEL 17 FUN-DRAISING DRIVE A SIGHT AND SOUND EXTRAVA-GANZA FOR THE LIFE OF YOUR CAR REAL FOOD FOR REAL PEOPLE A HIGH PRESSURE SYSTEM DISGUISED AS WORKERS FRANZ KLINE THE BISON HAVE ALL BUT DISAPPEARED I LOVE YOU PIZZA MAN REACH OUT AND TOUCH SOMEONE TODAY A HOSTAGE SITUATION I PITY THE FOOL 42nd STREET NOXZEMA DON'T WAIT ANOTHER MINUTE IN GENEVA I WANNA DANCE WITH

SOMEBODY JACK NICHOLSON THE OPTICAL DEPART-
MENT AT SEARS THE CHINESE AMBASSADOR YVES ST.
LAURENT'S NEW FALL LINE BOND JAMES BOND CAT
ON A HOT TIN ROOF THE SUPERSTATION HIYA CHIP
COME TO THINK OF IT I'LL HAVE A HEINEKEN THE
PRESIDENT OF THE UNITED STATES UNITED TO HA-
WAII ACT NOW SUBMITTED FOR YOUR APPROVAL
WHEN YOU WANT THE VERY BEST NEW FROM BURGER
KING WELL IT'S LIKE THIS BEAVER TEMPORARY RE-
LIEF OF MINOR SORE THROAT PAIN DOCTOR'S IN ROME
TONIGHT'S EDITORIAL DONNA IS CARRYING LARRY'S
BABY THE REVEREND JESSE JACKSON REMOVES THOSE
STUBBORN STAINS IN MINUTES NEW IMPROVED CAP-
TAIN WE HAVE A PROBLEM 37 TIMES ITS WEIGHT IN
EXCESS STOMACH ACID HILARIOUS ESCAPADES I'LL
TAKE MATHEMATICS FOR A HUNDRED PLEASE
HEEEEEEEERE'S JOHNNY ALL FOR ONLY $19.99.

During his speech in Mackey auditorium, Tom Sullivan, who
is blind and the subject of the film, "If You Could See What I
Hear," fell off the stage and into the orchestra pit. He was reaching
for a falling microphone and apparently lost his balance. He
suffered a fractured left wrist, which was temporarily treated with
an ice pack. He returned to finish his speech.

I come home late one night find you sitting on the couch
dressed like a boy hair pulled short no makeup. You want me to
leave I don't I go into the kitchen fix myself a brandy and soda.
You sit on the couch and stare at me through the kitchen door.
Someone knocks you let them in silently lead them upstairs. I hear
the bedroom door close softly. I go to the refrigerator to get ice for
my drink.

I realize the trick here is to laugh it off or wallow in self-pity
either one will dilute the emotion I get a drink bum a cigarette of

Art stand in the corner alone drinking and smoking can't anybody see me I'm so alone I need compassion I'm usually very good at this I watch people at the party I sneer but I don't leave Raoul comes up to me Do you believe in God No I say Do you believe in tragedy I don't answer well the greatest tragedy of living without God is that without God there can be no possibility of tragedy why don't you relax and come to Eva's with us.

Kirchner's Woman: What do I want, wanting to know you? What if I decided to define you as a force, and not as a person?

The Man: I take a role. I am the one who is going to cry: and I play this role for myself and it makes me cry: I am my own theater.

Kirchner's Woman: Love is obscene precisely because it puts the sentimental in place of the sexual.

The Man: I want to understand what is happening to me.

Kirchner's Woman: In order for me to show you where your desire is, it is enough for me to forbid you a little.

The Man: But isn't desire always the same whether the object is present or absent? Isn't the object always absent? I hallucinate what I desire.

Kirchner's Woman: He is in love, he creates meaning always and everywhere, out of nothing, and it is meaning which thrills him: he is in the crucible of meaning: a kind of festival not of the senses but of meaning.

THIS FATHER'S DAY, give him *ONE POLICE PLAZA,* a high adrenaline police novel loaded with action, violence and sex.

You want to get out of here, you talk to me.

Driving along the sharp blue streets in Sue's white mustang no fog tonight everything razor-sharp I'm sober too sober brutally slashing sober everything well-lit brightly illuminated the lines defined threatening the colors saturated fecund overripe the

41

shapes absolute geometric perfect the cityscape holding a gun to my consciousness Sally caresses my hand I smile sadly everyone in the car laughing and drinking Talking Heads on the radio it's a beautiful night I don't feel beautiful I feel ugly on purpose I want my pain to distinguish me.

Frances receives a note from Odets: My wife is returning. Your clothes are being sent to you. Do not attempt to contact me further. Goodbye, C.O.

The Devout, Desperate Wait For Statue To Cry For Them
Outside the church, an 11-year old girl who said she is a Presbyterian hawked photographs depicting a statue of the Virgin Mary to a crowd of gypsies. She wrestled with the question of whether it was a sin to make money from what many Chicagoans think is a miracle.
Nohemi Preciado had stood alongside her father, Carlos, as they worked the crowds of the curious, the devout and the desperate who had come to see the statue shed tears at St. John Catholic Church, 1234 W. 52nd Street.
"My father is a photographer and lives from selling pictures. The priest told us we could do it. We need the money."

The best French poetry since Baudelaire has been enlisted in a siege against the cliché. This has not been by any means a question of taste. It has been more a matter of life and death.

I know too much abundance of data not the lack of it that's my problem I know that Kirchner's Woman is leaving going back to her husband who once brilliantly poked tiny holes in her diaphragm with a pin there she is talking to Eva I smile say hi quickly grab a beer and sit on the couch she comes over sits next to me gives me a kiss on the cheek I think about the futility of all gestures the futility even of pain.

Mother's Day. Joe sits in the grass and thinks about his mother, sitting straight on the couch looking through the lowest lens of her trifocal glasses at the Reader's Digest, complaining bitterly about his father's affairs while he turned a deaf ear, trying to tell him about the facts of life when he was fifteen, falling asleep watching the news, looking ridiculous in the hospital, all puffy and swollen etc. Joe touches the cool engraved stone. He looks at the flowers he brought and cries a little.

PRISON FOR EX-LINEBACKER

Former Dallas Cowboy linebacker Thomas "Hollywood" Henderson was sentenced in Long Beach, CA to four years and eight months in prison for sexually assaulting two teenage girls and offering them a bribe to stop them from testifying. Henderson pleaded no contest to charges stemming from a November abduction and sexual assault on a 17-year-old quadrapalegic and her 15-year-old girlfriend.

"Nothing Outside of the Text"

Words/Music - Jane, Interruptus, Side, Jarr and Expressionism.

I've got	the language of love
I've got	the language of hate
It's all just	a way of speaking
No time	to hesitate
My words	go out to you
Your words	come back to me
Our words	control our lives
Without words	we cannot "be"

Demonstration Masturbation Regurgitation Blue
Isolation Determination Procrastination Jew
Elimination Dehydration Exaltation Sex
Nothing Nothing Nothing Outside of the Text
Metaphors abound
Symbols get me down
You know I just had to laugh

When I saw them hit the ground
I write   and what I write is good
You read   you read my words and think
You write   you write of many things
I read   I read your words and think
We create   the images of our life
We create   our personalities
We create   the words we need to use
We create   our own realities
Extreme Unction Mindless Function No Compunction Sign
Deconstruction Double Suction No Disjunction Line
Large Deduction Arms Reduction Reconstruction Next
Nothing, Nothing, Nothing Outside of the Text
fade

What's with you she asks Nothing not one goddamned thing I reply I guess you heard I'm returning to New York To get back with your husband let's not overlook that small detail He's my ex-husband but I'm going to give it another try she puts her tongue in my ears and whispers I want to sleep with you tonight I want to fuck you I turn to here and ask Are you always this affectionate or is it just the booze she stands up yells You asshole then turns and goes into the bathroom I honestly don't know what I am supposed to feel.

Sue Side and Art are both lying in bed, reading. Sue is reading *Penthouse* and Art is reading *ArtNews*. Without looking up, Sue says, "Hey Art, did you ever fantasize about raping me?"

Art puts his magazine down, "What?"

Sue, still reading, "Did you ever fantasize raping me? It says here that it's one of men's most common fantasies, raping some woman. There's this couple in here who really get off by pretending that the man's a burglar and he busts in and makes her do all kinds of things with him. C'mon Art, let's try it, c'mon Art, it'll be fun." She punches Art in the shoulder.

Art chuckles. "Sue, I really don't think we need all this theater just to get sexually aroused." He leans over and puts his hand on her knee. "I know I don't."

Sue grabs his wrist and puts his hand on the bed. "For Chrissakes Art, can't you loosen up a bit. C'mon, it'll be fun. I'll lie here and pretend I'm asleep, and you pretend you're a burglar, and you break in and try to rape me, and I'll resist and stuff, okay? Now c'mon, I'll lie here and pretend I'm asleep, and you go over there and pretend you're breaking in, okay?" Sue insistently pushes Art out of the bed.

Art reluctantly gets out of bed and walks over to the door. Sue turns over on her side and pretends she's asleep.

Art closes the door and starts walking over to the bed. "Turn the light out Art. Burglars work in the dark, not the light." Art retreats and flicks the switch off. He stealthily walks over to the bed and puts his hand over Sue's mouth. Sue struggles and softly bites his hand. Art throws the covers off the bed to expose Sue's body. Sue breaks his grip on her mouth. "No, no, leave me alone!" she screams.

"Huh?" Art relaxes. "I thought you wanted me to do this."

"Jesus Christ Art, I'm just pretending. Keep going, no matter what I say. And rough me up a bit, and talk dirty to me and stuff, okay?"

"I don't want to hurt you."

"You're not going to hurt me, I promise. C'mon, I'll pretend like I'm asleep again." Sue pulls the covers over her and lies on her side. Art obligingly starts anew.

"Hello bitch," he says, as again he puts his hand over her mouth. He removes his hand and kisses her roughly. She squirms out from his grasp and sits, breathing heavily, on the edge of the bed. "Get out of here or I'll scream." Art makes a move for her and she starts to run for the door. Art tackles her and roughly throws her on the bed.

"Ow."

"Are you okay?"

"Yes, yes, keep going. Help, help, police, somebody, heeelp! Who are you?"

"I'm a big black nigger and I'm going to fuck you good!" Art clumsily and slowly begins to undo her bra.

"Jesus Art, just rip it off, okay."

He rips it off and begins to kiss and fondle her breasts.

"No, no, no you bastard, you bastard, no."

"Shut your fucking mouth, or I'll really hurt you. Be a good little girl, and nobody gets hurt. All I want is a little white pussy."

Sue turns over on her stomach. "No, no, somebody help me, please help me."

"C'mon you little bitch, give it to me!" Art rips off her panties and inserts his knee between her legs. Sue's crotch is very wet.

"No, no, please don't." Art unbuttons his pants and opens Sue's legs.

"Now little whore, let's see what you got!" Art tries to enter Sue's vagina.

"No, no, please don't," Sue sobs.

"Am I hurting you?" asks Art.

"No, I'm just playing. No, no, don't," she screams, and she rises up a little to make it easier for Art to enter her.

Art tries to enter her. "C'mon, you bitch," he says, without conviction.

"No, no you monster, you black bastard, you animal, no, no," says Sue, while Art is still trying to enter her.

"You fucking whore, you slut,"Art says. He still can't get it in.

"What's wrong?" Sue asks.

"I dunno. I can't get hard," says Art.

"Great!" says Sue.

Died: Michel Foucault, 57, one of France's most prominent philosophers and teachers, of a neurological disorder in Paris, June 25.   Foucault, a leader of the philosophical school of structuralism, explored Western culture's approach to madness, sexuality, crime and punishment. The second and third volumes of his unfinished "History of Sexuality" were published less than two weeks before his death; in the third he maintains that women have been oppressed by men in all societies throughout history.

Sally and Raoul come sit next to me on the couch Look at the people dancing says Raoul one eye on the mirror and the other eye looking for the video camera the trouble with people today is that everyone used to want to star in their own movies now they all want to star in their own rock videos You're right says Sally No I don't think I am says Raoul Do you know one reason Kirchner's Woman is leaving Sally asks me To get back with her husband I say Yeah but do you know why it's because her husband is loaded filthy rich Oh I say but I think she loves me I protest Those who choose love over money have experienced neither says Raoul.

Sally has a dream. In this dream she's driving down a long country road with her brother and some of his friends. It's spring, and they're surrounded by rolling green hills, strong brown horses and the heavy scents of livestock and wet grass. She smiles at her brother's friend who is sitting next to her in the front seat. He smiles back and puts his hand on her thigh. Sally feels surprised and flattered. He slowly moves his hand up her thigh to her crotch. Sally begins to get excited. She looks at him looking out the window and feels his hand rubbing her crotch. All of a sudden the car is rolling. In slow motion they turn over once, twice, three times. Sally is thrown from the car. She gets up, shakes herself off, and begins walking toward the car, which has landed on its top a few yards down the road. As she nears the vehicle, she sees the dismembered arms and legs of her brother and his friends lying bloody in the road. She sees the stump of the hand that was caressing her, cut off at the elbow. Sally wakes up feeling disgusted and ferociously aroused.

HOW TO HELP A LITTLE GIRL MAKE IT ALL THE WAY TO 7.

It wasn't long ago that if little Kamala Rama drank the water in her village she would have taken her life in her hands.

Today, thanks to *Save The Children*, she can have clean water to wash with, and fresh water for her mother to cook with.

And she can do something else that was once unheard of in her village for a little girl.

She can go to school. Even past the fifth grade.

Please won't you help. Send the coupon today.

There are still so many children who need the chance Kamala Rama got.

The chance to make it to 7.

125. He spreads a powerful glue upon the rim of a privy seat and sends the girl in to shit; directly she sits down, her ass is caught fast. Meanwhile, from the other side a small charcoal brazier is introduced beneath her ass. Scorched, she leaps up, leaving almost a perfect circle of skin behind her.

Now what I ask Raoul now what do I do About what he asks About Kirchner's Woman I can only tell you what I would do my boy and I would do absolutely nothing I have no desire for anyone that is why people flock to me I have achieved the perfect state of grace for our time I am permanently languid Sally laughs You are so full of shit Raoul it's amazing Yes it is amazing but one needs to realize that conversation and making love are similar both are extreme acts of survival which create their own truth and neither is absolutely necessary I get up to find Kirchner's Woman.

Joe is enamoured with Frances has been for some time. He saves his money finally asks her out to an expensive French restaurant, *Le Tromp L'Oeil*. She accepts. Joe is happy nervous buys flowers cleans his suit the whole nine yards. He doesn't know anything about wine he worries about this. During the *apéritif* and *le consommé de poulet aux petits légumes* they get acquainted How are you Fine Isn't the *paté* delicious Yes it is etc..

During *le petit filet de porc en brioche sauce poivrade* Frances begins to talk about Odets. How she loves him how she hates him how she can't live with him how she can't live without him. This musing becomes a monologue which continues through *le civet de lapin au marc de bourgogne* past *l'ommelette norvégienne* and clear up to *le café et le digestif* Joe can't get a word in edgewise. Joe is hurt and angry but he listens he wants to be a good person. He is disappointed in the evening the food was very good but he's weary. He does not want to pay the whole check he doesn't think he should have to. Frances reaches for the check but Joe stops her he wants to do the right thing. "This is my treat," he says. Frances is pleased she stops talking and looks at Joe. "That was very sweet," she says and smiles at him, "thank you." Joe smiles back and they touch hands across the table. Frances takes a drink of wine and starts telling Joe about her and Odet's' sex life.

"A dear little lady who does everything from the goodness of her heart" is an apt description of Ada Mae Goodell.

Goodell is that rare soul who never minded doing for others. For many years she has done so by an unusual service: trimming the toenails of the elderly and infirm persons who cannot do this little chore for themselves. The ritual includes soaking the feet, removing ingrown nails, filing as well as trimming. She has never charged for this service, but is occasionally the recipient of gifts from her "clients."

Goodell has earned so little that she qualifies for very little in Social Security benefits. Nevertheless, she lives well on what she does receive. She says, "What would I do with new and fancy clothes? They wouldn't even look right on me."

The word from outside is
She's on the ledge again
Drawing a crowd and
Threatening everything
I'm here wondering

Just where I fit in
Everybody says I don't care
No I don't care
I'm just trying to remember
The Days of Wine and Roses

I knock on the bathroom door It's me let me in What do you want I want to talk with you I want to apologize after a few seconds the door opens a crack this is just like All My Children I want to talk with you the door opens all the way I notice she's been crying I sit on the edge of the tub she sits on the stool her face in her hands we don't speak then she looks up at me What do you want from me I want to make love with you tonight I say I kiss her hands Why she asks Haven't we been through this before I answer we both laugh What do you want from me I ask I want us to be friends she says Fuck you I say.

Sweet Jane's 10 All Time Favorite Movies
1) Joan of Arc - Ingrid Bergeman.
2) Entre Nous
3) Lili Marlene
4) The 4th Man
5) Who's Afraid of Virginia Woolf?
6) What Ever Happened to Baby Jane?
7) Liquid Sky
8) The Stationmaster's Wife
9) A Woman in Flames
10) Road Warrior

Consider the case of Lillie Frierson, 13, of Los Angeles. Michael Jackson doesn't eat meat, neither does Lillie. Michael sleeps on a mat on the floor. So did Lillie, until her mother ordered her back into bed. Michael wears beaded jackets. So does Lillie, a $350 red one that her mother, Doris, bought for her birthday. "I must be as crazy as she is," Doris sighs. "I hope that nothing ever happens to him because if it does, that child is going to need to have help."

The people of the earth will now - perhaps - be set free. But I must go. This is sad and death is hard. But no harder than my life has been, at which so many people took offense. After my death, sooner or later, they will surely sing my praises and admire my art. Will they do it as immoderately as they have abused, ridiculed, scorned and neglected me and my work? Possibly. There will always be misunderstandings between me and others. I care neither one way nor the other.

I don't understand she says I don't understand the point you're trying to make You don't want to understand Okay maybe I don't maybe all I want to do is to get the fuck out of here get away from everything and everyone including you all I want to do is to eat drink and sleep and not have to worry about anything not have to worry about money or where my next meal is coming from I want to go back to my husband's very expensive and very large bed and pull the covers up over my head I can't deal with anyone else's demands expectations or problems I don't want to think or feel I just want to eat sleep and drink can you understand that can you.

"Our first guest, as you know if you were listening, is La Galoue, the new model who is fast becoming the rage of Paris, New York, and eastern Tazmania. Welcome La Galoue. Can I call you 'La?'"
"You can call me anything you want, David."
"Well, thank you. Ha Ha Ha. You are indeed a very lovely lady, La Galoue. La Galoue, that's a very, well, strange name. What does it mean, if I may be so bold to ask?"
"It means 'The Glutton,' Dave."
"The Glutton, huh. Okay. And would you please inform our viewers how a lovely lady like yourself came to called, well, let's

be frank, a rather unflattering name like 'The Glutton.'"

"Well, David, once at this restaurant I ate a hundred sausages, in one night."

"You ate a hundred sausages in ONE NIGHT!!! I see. Ha Ha. Well, La Galoue, we at the David Letterman show, what are you laughing at Paul, we at the David Letterman show have spared no expense to bring to our audience the finest in television entertainment, while publicly humiliating as many people as possible. If you would be so kind as to step over here my dear, you will see that we have a table set up with bowls filled with over two hundred pork and beef sausages, fully cooked and ready to eat, mmm, mmm. And when we come back, we are going to have a sausage eating contest, between our own Larry 'Bud' Mehlman, myself, and you, the lovely La Galoue, to see who can eat the most of those beauties in five minutes. When we return, after this message, we'll find out who the real glutton is here. After this."

New Pepsi Light - Life just keeps on getting better!

What is this man, a detective, a floorwalker, or a poet?
While all three, and pretty good at making love too, eh my dear?

I was really hoping we wouldn't end up hating each other I guess I underestimated both of us do you know what your trouble is she asks me No you tell me what my trouble is Your trouble is that you have absolutely no idea of what you want I know exactly what I want it's just that the things I want are mutually exclusive do you find doomed men attractive Yes and no what do you mean by mutually exclusive Well for example I want to be with you yet I want to be happy maybe the greatest freedom we have is choosing our own particular hell.

Joe had a girlfriend once. They got along really well, had a great sex life, and lived together for almost a year. Then one day she went crazy and tried to kill herself. This was the most important thing that ever happened to Joe. He now lives the life of a grieving widower, he has appropriated her suicide attempt into his own personality. Joe has based his life on another person's problems. He is not sure if he even has a set of neuroses he can truly call his own.

While I'm writing this letter to *Penthouse*, you might be interested to know that my wife is in the bedroom lying on the bed. She has a vibrator in her vagina and one in her rectum and both are turned on. And, of course, she is tied spreadeagled to the bed and gagged.

Bill, my neighbor, approved when he came over to look at her, and I found his wife a real turn-on as she hung from a hook in their basement ceiling, her hands over her head, her vibrators also turned on. I'm not sure when I'm going to let my wife go free, but you can bet it will cost her. There are still a lot of things that need to be done.

Mr. (Name and address withheld)

Before any action, the urban guerilla must think of the methods and personnel at his disposal to carry out the action. Operations and actions that demand the urban guerilla's technical preparations cannot be carried out by someone who lacks that technical skill. With these cautions, the action models which the urban guerilla can carry out are the following: assaults; raids and penetrations; occupation; ambush; street tactics; strikes and work interruptions; desertions; diversions; seizures, expropriations of arms; ammunition and explosives; liberation of prisoners; executions; kidnappings; sabotage; terrorism; armed propaganda; war of nerves.

It's getting late she says I'd better go she gets up off the stool opens the bathroom door Can I come with you I ask she looks at me for awhile Why not she sighs we leave the party step out into the cold night air it's almost dawn I hold her hand she turns to face me What do I want wanting to know you she asks.

When I arrived at Kirchner's Woman's apartment on Wednesday it was seven o'clock exactly. Since I didn't want to appear too eager I decided to walk around the block. She lived in a nice neighborhood, right off Nob Hill, but her apartment building looked pretty trashed, at least from the outside. I walked slowly around the block and was back at her door at about seventeen after, just late enough. I knocked on the door and this other women answered. She invited me in and I sat on the couch. She was very pretty, stunning in fact. I asked her if Kirchner's Woman was there and she said "Well I hate to sink your ship burst your bubble shatter your dreams put a crimp in your plans rain on your parade sack your capital block your kick rip your rubber scratch your record erase your space piss in your sink rustle your cattle put a run in your nylons spill your drink strafe your village split your atom torpedo your tanker embargo your oil capture your embassy soil your sheets torture your cat sodomize your younger brother smoke your last joint strike you out puke on your pillow double you up burn your toast spoil your debut stop you at the line of scrimmage scratch your paint foreclose your mortgage mine your harbor break your mirror rob you of extra bases nuke your whales ruin your day hit you where it counts eat your honey spit in your beer shoot your horse break your crown oppress your masses stand in your light ring your bell bust your balls fart in your face spill your beans lose your marbles tip your scales slit your throat pierce your ears crash your party rain on your parade screw you blue shit in your shoes fuck your mother and your sister twice. . . but she just left. However, she did leave this note."

POLICE SEEK PERSON WHO YELLED "JUMP" TO SUICIDE

Brownsville, PA, (AP) - Police said Monday they were seeking a person who shouted "Jump!" moments before a distraught man leaped to his death.

The death of Samuel Holmes of Brownsville was the second suicide during the weekend from the 175-foot high Lane-Bane Bridge.

Police said Holmes was bringing his other leg back over the rail to stand on the sidewalk when someone on the railroad tracks yelled "Jump!"

Holmes stood up, looked at his taunter, glanced back at the officer and stepped off the railing. "Perhaps... if no one had said 'jump' it would have saved his life," a police spokesman said.

POST-NUKE THRILL FREAKS LOOKING FOR A KICK!

Jesus what time is it she says sitting up quickly in bed god I've got a terrible headache Comes from drinking way too much and passing out I say Did I do that she looks at me I'm terribly sorry last night was supposed to be special We can try for this morning I say I kiss her on the mouth she kisses me back then pushes me away I've got to be at the airport in an hour So you'll miss your flight No I can't do that she gets up out of bed goes to the bathroom I can't believe this is happening to me.

La Galoue has been hired to be the model for Toujour Deja Parfum. Her first ad will appear in the next issues of *Elle*, *Mademoiselle*, and *Vogue*.

Partygoer Who Left Car Home Dies
A man who knew he would be drinking at a weekend party decided not to drive, only to be killed as he hitchhiked home when an allegedly drunken driver ran him down on an approach ramp to an interstate.

That was all she dreamed about, escape. She saw herself at night, running naked down a highway, running across fields, running down riverbeds. Always running. And always just when she was about to get away, he would be there. And he would stop her somehow. He would just appear, and stop her.
And when she told him these dreams, he believed them. He knew she had to be stopped, or she would leave him forever. So he tied a cowbell to her ankle, so he could hear at night if she tried

to get out of bed. But she learned how to muffle the bell by stuffing a sock into it, and inching her way out of the bed, and into the night. He caught her one night when the sock fell out and he heard her trying to run to the highway. He caught her, and dragged her back to the trailer, and tied her to the stove with his belt. He just left her there, and went back to bed, and lay there listening to her scream. Then he listened to his son scream. And he was surprised at himself, because he didn't feel anything anymore. All he wanted to do was. . . sleep. And for the first time, he wished he were far away. Lost in a deep, vast country, where nobody knew him. Somewhere without language, or streets. And he dreamed about this place without knowing its name. And when he woke up, he was on fire.

I sit on the edge of Kirchner's Woman's bed and watch her pack Well I say this is it can I go with you to the airport No I'd rather you didn't Why not I'd prefer a clean break you know as least sticky as possible god damn you don't look at me like that you're so fucking naive you just can't understand can you that people will do anything and I mean anything just to survive emotionally and it's not like I promised you anything either we haven't even known each other for very long so please get that puppy dog look off your face it just makes me want to laugh.

Sweet Jane, Sally and Frances go to *The Gilded Cage* for a drink.

"Why are you so depressed?" Sally asks Frances.

"It's Odets. We were supposed to go dancing last night and he never showed up. Didn't even call. I feel like shit."

"That's too bad," Sally says. "Why didn't you give me a call, we could have gone for a drink or something."

"I love him, I really do, but he treats me so bad. He treats me like shit, all the time."

"Why do you put up with that crap?" Sweet Jane loudly asks. "Why don't you tell him to go fuck himself pronto? That's what

I'd do if some asshole tried to treat me like that."

"You don't understand."

"What's there to understand? You've fallen for a cruel, manipulative jerk, let's face it. Not to mention he's married, too. And instead of saying 'Fuck you pal, go take a hike,' you blame yourself, you fall back on words like 'I love him' and 'But he's a genius.' You can't rationalize that shit to me, so don't even try. Unless . . ." Sweet Jane winks at Frances, "you get off on being shat upon."

"That wasn't necessary," says Sally.

"Hey, who knows, maybe she's the kind that digs being stood up and fucked around. You know what I think, St. Frances the Martyr, I think you loved being crucified, I think you adore it."

Frances looks at Sweet Jane and chuckles. "Who are you to talk to me about courage and desire? You haven't been tickled, licked, played with or fucked since I've known you. I don't think you even masturbate. So don't talk to me about love or desire. You're just like Raoul, you think because you don't feel anything you know everything. But that's just not true."

'Fat Lips' Look Touts Pouts

New York - Scores of women are lining up to get fat lips, paying $300 a pop for the "pouty," sensuous look quickly created by collagen injections, a Manhattan plastic surgeon said Thursday.

The "fuller and sexier" look in lips is the latest rage, said Dr. Robert Vitolo. Injecting collagen - a protein derived from cow skin - into the upper lip takes only minutes.

A story? No. No stories, never again.

I'm sorry she says I didn't mean that it's just that I'm rather on edge you see That's okay I say Let's play a game she says come over here let's look into each other's eyes and tell each other exactly what we see okay no lying just honesty brutal honesty come over here you go first I look deeply into her eyes see the black surrounded by the deep green surrounded by the white I see a little bit of fear I say plus you look very tired almost resigned Is that all she asks I nod Okay my turn she looks deep into my eyes I see despair in your eyes she says at last despair and hope too and there's something else I see but I can't really tell exactly what it is.

"Hello darlings. You've reached La Galoue's personal phone number. I'm not home right now, but if you'd be so kind as to leave a message, I'd simply love to get back to you as soon as I can. *Au revoir.*"

"*Allo. C'est Henri. Je voudrais vous voir bientôt, okay? Téléphonez-moi s'il vous plaît.*"

Hi. This is not Cathy, this is only a recording of Cathy's voice. Cathy's not here, she'll return on Wednesday. If you want to leave a message, be my guest, but remember, I'm not Cathy, I'm just a machine."

"*Bonjour. C'est Henri. Téléphonez-moi.*"

"I'm Sue. I'm Jennifer. And I'm Sarah. We can't come to the phone right now. But please leave a message and one of us will call you as soon as we can. Wait for the beep. Bye now."

"Jennifer, this is Henri. Please call me."

"Hi, I'm Prudence, Julie's answering machine. You can tell me anything, and I promise I'll tell Julie when she gets home. If she ever does get home, that slut. You can even talk dirty to me, I like that."

Toulouse hangs up the phone and closes his address book. He puts his coat on and goes out in the direction of *Le Petit Trou.* Hopefully Marie will be there.

A sample from our catalogue:
"Slash and Thrust," a knifer-fighting manual for the novice.
"I Hate You! (An Angry Man's Guide to Revenge)."
"Bare Kills," a training course of killing without weapons.

"Sneak it Through - Smuggling Made Easy."
"The100 Deadliest Karate Moves."
"Hit Man (A Technical Volume for the Independent Contractor)."
"How to Kill" (5 Volumes).
BOOKS DON'T KILL PEOPLE - PEOPLE KILL PEOPLE

Mayest thou never exist, may thy ka never exist, may thy body never exist.

May thy limbs never exist.	May thou never exist.
May thy bones never exist.	May thou never exist.
May thy words of power never exist.	May thou never exist.
Mayest thou never exist.	May thou never exist.
May thy form never exist.	May thou never exist.
May thy attributes never exist.	May thou never exist.
May that which springs from thee never exist	May thou never exist.
May thy hair never exist.	May thou never exist.
May thy possessions never exist.	May thou never exist.
May thy emissions never exist.	May thou never exist.
May the material of thy body never exist.	May thou never exist.
May thy place never exist.	May thou never exist.
May thy tomb never exist.	May thou never exist.
May thy cavern never exist.	May thou never exist.
May thy funereal chamber never exist.	May thou never exist.
May thy paths never exist.	May thou never exist.
May thy seasons never exist.	May thou never exist.
May thy words never exist.	May thou never exist.
May thy enterings never exist.	May thou never exist.
May thy journeys never exist.	May thou never exist.
May thy advancings never exist.	May thou never exist.
May thy comings never exist.	May thou never exist.
May thy sitting down never exist.	May thou never exist.
May thy increase never exist.	May thou never exist.
May thy body never exist.	May thou never exist.

May thy prosperity never exist.   May thou never exist.
Thou art smitten, O enemy, Thou shalt die, thou shalt die.
Thou shalt perish, thou shalt perish, thou shalt perish.

It seems like we're always talking in circles I say we just talk in circles and we never say anything Isn't that from a movie she asks I'm sorry she sighs heavily it seems as if we can't help hurting each other doesn't it she pauses for a second we all have this emotional baggage we've collected through the years each time we brush up against somebody they hand us another piece of luggage so we've got our problems and their problems and problems of what to do with all this baggage so we start to look for someone we can dump all this on but everybody's hands are full with their own stuff that's what love is trying to dump your past luggage on someone But everyone wants to be loved we just go about it in different ways Not me I don't want to be loved my hands are too full right now she says.

Sweet Jane and Sally have joined a band of women and men who call themselves *The Feministas.* Some of them have permits to carry guns. They have this hotline, and any time an abortion clinic is being threatened or picketed, they drive over and protect the clinic, sometimes with force. Sweet Jane almost got hit in the head with a brick once. She really digs the group.

Happiness turned to heartbreak when truck driver Stuart Kelly won an $11 million lottery, then learned he had terminal cancer.
The Ontario, Canada man died just months after winning the biggest jackpot in the country's history.

I don't have anything
Except for your electric chair
I don't have anything
Except for the shit you put in my hair
I don't have anything

Except for your alarm clock
I don't have anything
That wakes me up to nothing but the walls
I don't have anything
I don't have anything
Watch out for the furniture

You've never been really desperate have you I ask I'm desperate right now she says I'm leaving someone I like very much in order to be with someone else whom I hate simply because I'm very tired of having no money I'd say that was a very desperate gesture wouldn't you You mean if I had money you'd stay here No there's more to it than that I just can't bear to be loved right now I desperately want to be left alone the phone rings she sneers I can't even get the fuck out of here without everyone I know interrupting I make my way to the door.

Joe, Frances, Sally, Raoul and I are sitting at *The Turkey Baster* having sandwiches and drinks. Joe is telling us this story he read in a magazine about some dyslexic black guy from the South Bronx who won a scholarship to Harvard and who now owns a $3 million dollar software company in Massachusetts.

"Wow, a dyslexic black from the South Bronx, how marginal can you get?" I say.

"He's still a male. If he were a she, then you'd have a story," says Frances.

"Or if it was an American Indian, or Eskimo," says Raoul.

"What about this, a black ex con with AIDS?"

"How about a blind, black, ex-con with AIDS?"

"How about a gay, blind, black ex-con with AIDS, who uses drugs, prays to Allah, and was convicted of raping a white woman?"

"How about a blind, black, gay ex-con junkie with AIDS, who was arrested for child-molesting,but who got off on a technicality?"

"A 50 year old pregnant Navaho who has never been married, who has never had a job, is an AIDS carrier, has seven children besides, is illiterate and deaf."

"And who lives with her lesbian lover."

"And who has to use crutches."

"And who has a brain tumor."

"C'mon, I'm trying to eat."

I'm Martha Quinn and you're watching MTV, America's Rock Music Channel. Coming up in about half an hour, we've got Mark Goodman and the Music News, and in about fifteen minutes, we're going to give you some tour information for The Boss, Bruce Springsteen. All that after this, a word from our friends at Starburst.

The trouble with great literature is that any asshole can identify with it.

Wait she calls back to me it's for you it's Sally Frances has been arrested What a terrible inconvenience for you I mutter as I pick up the phone she gives me the finger and turns to finish packing hello Hello this is Sally Frances has been arrested Where Up North somewhere For what DWI She doesn't drive anymore I know it must be that old warrant maybe she didn't take care of it you know how she is always waiting until the last minute or forgetting completely Have you spoken to her No her lawyer called he said she really flipped out called the police cocksuckers and all kinds of names Exactly where is she They're holding her in some town called Mendocino up on the coast Can you pick me up here I'm supposed to take Kirchner's Woman to the airport She can take a cab pick me up here as soon as you can.

Sally likes Joe who likes Frances who likes Odets who is married.

La Galoue likes everybody but especially Toulouse-Lautrec who likes Sweet Jane who likes Raoul who doesn't like anybody except maybe me who likes Kirchner's Woman who is married. To Odets.

Art likes Sue Side who likes Curtis Interruptus (the drummer) who likes Sally who likes Joe etc.

Parents of Teen Say Drugs Made Him Kill

Devil worship, hallucinogenic drugs and rock music led "the greatest kid in the world" to ritual murder and suicide at the end of a jailhouse bedsheet, the parents of 17-year-old Richard Kasso said Monday.

The young Kasso, accused by police of the ritual mutilation murder last month of a East Northport teenager, was found hanged in his Suffolk County jail cell early Saturday, hours after his arraignment on second degree murder charges.

Kasso's parents said their son was devastated by hallucinogenic drugs.

"He told us, 'I enjoy the fantasy world of drugs. You can't stop me. I love drugs,'" said his father, a high school social studies teacher.

Authorities claim Kasso was involved in the "Knights of the Black Circle," a group of perhaps 20 teenagers who allegedly took drugs and tortured animals in Satanic rituals.

Kasso and James Troiano, 18, were charged in the ritual murder of Gary Lauwers, 17.

That is why modern art divides the public into two classes, those who understand it and those who do not understand it - that is to say, those who are artists and those who are not. The new art is an artistic art.

I put down the phone sit back on the edge of the bed Is Frances in trouble she asks me Yes she's been arrested and she's flipping out Sally won't be able to drive you to the airport you'll have to take a cab Do you have some money I could borrow for the taxi I can only spare five we might have to buy gas Kirchner's Woman finishes packing closes her suitcase stares out the window What are you thinking she asks me I'm thinking about Frances I hope her mother doesn't have her committed like she did a couple of years ago I turn to look at her What are you thinking I ask her I'm thinking about Frances and about you and about how incredibly thirsty I am she moves over to her dresser Do you mind if I play some music No not at all she turns on the cassette.

I looked at the note and then folded it up and put it in my pocket. Kirchner's Woman's Roommate was smiling at me provocatively. "Anything I can do?" she asked.

"No, thank you. Your roommate wrote she'd return soon, so I'll just wait here if that's okay with you."

"That's more than fine with me. Can I get you a beer?"

"That would be nice, thanks."

"Kirchner's Woman tells me you're a comedian, that sounds like a lot of fun."

"It's all right. It's hard to get jobs though, it seems like everyone's a comedian these days. Where do you work?"

"In North Beach. I'm an 'exotic dancer.' There's always jobs for that. I'm also a grad student at Berkeley."

"Oh yeah, what are you studying?"

"Philosophy."

Lingerie does a lot for a woman. Not to mention what it does for a man. I love a woman who says how she feels. But I also love a woman who has secrets. In fact, it's what she keeps to herself that says the most about her. Lingerie. That's a secret she doesn't share with the world. So sometimes you don't find out. But then again, sometimes you do.

We have only to be lucky once— you have to be lucky always.

She sits down on the bed facing the door we don't speak I kiss the back of her neck feel her tiny hairs on my tongue When will I see you again I ask her she doesn't say anything I nibble her left ear lobe she turns to face me You're not making this any easier she says I don't want to make it easier I want to make it harder I want to make it impossible for you to leave me You can't do that you can only make it somewhat more difficult no matter how much you try you can only slightly fuck things up she gets up from the bed I'm going to New York I have my ticket she digs in her bag pulls out an airline ticket thrusts it in my face see I'm going and there's not one goddamn thing you can do about it do you understand not one goddamn thing you can do you're only a bit player here you don't have a major part and this is our final scene so goodbye the music's still playing she closes her eyes and slumps down on the bed I want to slap her but it's not worth the effort I hear Sally's car honk in the street.

Okay let's go in Tonight *The Stained Sheet* proudly presents Mink Whip Mannequins For Jesus and Danny and the Derrideans Two Twenty dollars thank you Hi Toulouse have you seen Patricia No we've just arrived Hey watch it asshole Fuck you pal We had a couple of cases of beer and some really good crank and we got wasted man and Leper was there and she wanted to fuck Veggie but Veggie blew cookies all over Anton's couch and No no you forget that Levi-Strauss was actually referring to Jesus look at this is that a girl or a boy Where Over there by the bathrooms I'm working on this collage with grocery receipts and dog food labels Jeanine how are you you look so cool can I bum a ciggie Where's my gun where's my gun where's my gun cuz I gotta cum Yeah I saw Stillborn here they were great This is my friend Terry we call her Miss Piggy Why do you call her that I dunno cuz she looks like a pig Let's go sit down What I said let's go sit down Okay Yeah I did go through what you might call a junky phase Hey buddy loan me a buck to buy a beer I got stains in my underwear and I'm thinking bout you thinking bout you thinking bout you you you you you Who is this band they suck I saw them at the *Bleeding Squirrel* they were a lot Hi what can I get for you tonight What Do you want anything to drink Yes please cognac for me and a gin and tonic for her What Brandy for me and a gin and tonic for the lady Okay be back in a sec I just can't believe she would say a thing like that Aw she's a clit forget her What did you say Nothing not a thing Thank you God I need earplugs What I said God I need earplugs Oh Who is this band anyway What Who is this band onstage I still can't hear you I SAID WHO THE FUCK IS THIS BAND ONSTAGE Mink Whip What MINK WHIP they're from New York Oh Hey man gotta quarter No I'm sorry How bout you honey gotta quarter Here buddy here's a quarter now leave us alone Thanks man Jesus was a lapdog eats like a fucking hog Jesus is slugbait never had to masturbate No I have never read Baudrillard LA GALOUE BENNY oh Sweetheart how are you Oh just fine I saw your poster the other day quite the sensation Thank you oh Benny have you met Toulouse-Lautrec Yeah man a few times how ya doin' Fine would you like to sit down What Okay let me get my purse Henri we'll be back in a second C'mon Marty let's get another drink Look asshole I don't want to dance why don't you just go fuck yourself I saw the Big Chill last night on cable I just adore Rimbaud too Thank you goodnight Off the stage assholes YEAAAAAAAAAA FUCK YOU YEAAAAAAAAAA Let's hear it for Mink Whip Y E A A A A A A A A A A H H H H H H H F U U U U U C K YOOOOOUUUU Shit they were horrible Booooooooooo Yeaaaaaaaaa Jesus I hope they don't do an encore Anybody sitting here friend Yes You sure Yes I'm quite sure Bobby guess what What I got a job Great where at You'll never believe it Try me Ma Bell I'm a telephone operator.

Woman Found Shot to Death on S.F. Beach

A 32-year-old San Francisco woman apparently shot herself to death in a sleeping bag on Baker Beach early yesterday morning after leaving a suicide note saying that she had used a gun because guns are easier to get than drugs, police said.

U.S. Parks service detective Dan Kellison said that the woman's body was found by a beach walker about 9 am yesterday. She had been shot once in the head with a .32 caliber pistol that was found with the body.

For example, many persons in the time of this visitation never perceived they were infected till they found, to their unspeakable surprise, the tokens come out upon them: after which they seldom lived six hours, for those spots they called the tokens were really gangrene spots, or mortified flesh in small knobs, as broad as a silver penny, and as hard as a piece of callus or horn; so that, when the disease was come up to that length, there was nothing could follow but certain death, and yet, as I said, they knew nothing of their being infected, not found themselves so much out of order, till those mortal marks were upon them.

Well I say I guess this is it Yeah I guess so she says You have nothing to say to me I ask her No not really she shakes her head this ain't no movie Will I ever see you again Why do you persist in living in the cliché just let it go please just let it go Clichés are all I can have left christ this is bad dialogue I'm standing facing the door I can hear Sally's horn honking again and again I'm waiting for some sort of climax some sort of resolution some sort of closure I need to get on with my life Kirchner's Woman says nothing Sally honks her horn I stare at the door she continues to say nothing nothing.

Thank you very much, thank you very much, you're much too kind, thank you, thank you, no really thank you. Well it's good to be back at *The Cafe Zero*, it's been a while since I've been here, well anyway we'll have some fun tonight, have a few drinks, a few chuckles, maybe some of us will get laid tonight, would you like that? Sure you would, sure you would. Say, didja hear about the guy with five penises? His pants fit him like a glove. Oh how I love cheap laughs.

Mastercard - I'm bored.

The City Tramp, The Little Chaos, Love is Colder Than Death, Katzelmacher, Gods of the Plague, Why does Herr R. Run Amok? Rio Das Mortes, The Coffee House, Whity, The Nicklashausen Journey, The American Soldier, Beware of a Holy Whore, Pioneers in Ingolstadt, Merchant of the Four Seasons, The Bitter Tears of Petra von Kant, Wild Game, Eight Hours Are Not a Day, Bremen Coffee, World on a Wire, Nora Helmer, Fear Eats the Soul, Martha, Effie Briest, Fox, Like a Bird on a Wire, Mother Kusters' Journey to Heaven, Fear of Fear, I Only Want You to Love Me, Satan's Brew, Chinese Roulette, The Station Master's Wife, Women in New York, Despair, Germany in Autumn, The Marriage of Maria Braun, In a Year With 13 Moons, The Third Generation, Berlin Alexanderplatz, Lili Marlene, Lola, Theatre in a Trance, Veronika Voss, Querelle.

That fucking bitch I say as I get into Sally's car that fucking cunt I hate that word Sally says I think it might be the only obscene word left I'm sorry I say but that scene just now the way she wouldn't talk to me wouldn't even say goodbye that was an obscenity I don't mean to be an asshole but that's no excuse Jesus Sally lighten up the whole world's nothing but one big cesspool and you get upset about one little word Some of the world is obscene that's true but I'm not sure obscenity is an appropriate reaction look what's happening to Frances Okay I'm sorry I won't say another word any more I'm sorry too that one word just bothers me.

"So you study philosophy, huh? That must be exciting."
"It's okay. It seems like I read all of the time."
"What philosophers do you enjoy reading?"

"I like Kierkegaard, and Heidegger and. . . " Kirchner's Woman's Roommate moved closer to me on the couch, "Nietzsche and Husserl. . . " she put her arms around me and began to kiss my face, "And of course Parmenides and the pre-socratics. . . " she kissed me on the lips and put her tongue in my mouth. I think I heard her try to mumble "Descartes" as her hands moved down to my pants and started to unbuckle my belt. Just then we heard the front door unlock. Kirchner's Woman's Roommate jumped back as Kirchner's Woman walked in.

You got the raise.
The one that was due over six months ago.
You called your wife to tell her the news.
When you got home there was an official-looking envelope waiting for you.
You opened it, showed it to your wife, and poured two Christian Brothers.
You'd won the state lottery.
Cheers.

The deconstruction is not something we have added to the text but it constituted the text in the first place. A literary text simultaneously asserts and denies the authority of its own rhetorical mode, and by reading the text as we did we were only trying to come closer to being as rigorous a reader as the author had to be in order to write the sentence in the first place. Poetic writing is the most advanced and refined mode of deconstruction; it may differ from critical or discursive writing in the economy of its articulation, but not in kind.

You've really fallen for her haven't you Sally says as we speed along the highway Why how can you tell It seems like you've changed a little bit Nobody ever changes here I say we all stay the same You don't know her very well do you I mean you haven't known her for very long have you No only a couple of weeks I knew her back when I lived in Colorado we were pretty good friends Oh yeah I didn't know that you don't seem to be very chummy any more No we're not Mind if I ask why You can ask but I don't think I'll tell you Oh we drive along in silence for a few miles One thing I can tell you though is that I wouldn't worry about not seeing her again she cracks up every six months or so and goes back to Odets then she leaves him they can't stand each other I bet she's back before the summer's over I didn't know that I thought she really hated it here The only thing she hates is penury Why didn't you tell me this before I was hoping you wouldn't get so involved with her Why I don't want to talk about it any more we drive on to rescue Frances.

FALLING STARS
A performance with accompanying text recreating the deaths of five major celebrities. Once again Art gives the public what it wants.
    Part I - Marilyn Monroe
    Part II - John Wayne
    Part III - Elvis Presley
    Part IV - Janis Joplin
    Part V - Liberace

IBM, the world's largest computer company, said its profits rose 202 percent in the third quarter, compared to last year.

A desires B.
A believes B is magic.
B is magic good and bad. A is magic also that is A can see magic where none exists.

Do you mind if I turn on the radio I ask her No not at all as long as we don't have to listen to the news I turn the knob and tune in an old rhythm and blues station the landscape rushes by the day is pleasant warm but not hot Today is a good day not to die I say What

Sally asks me why did you say that you know you should work in a hospital for a couple of days see the things I see maybe actually witnessing some real pain and suffering might dent that cool ironic shield I wasn't being ironic all I said was that today is a good day not to die Sally laughed you know for a comedian you're not very profound So I've heard and for a nurse you're not very compassionate You don't need pity what you need is a good fuck Don't we all I say.

"So, I see you've met my roommate."

"We've been discussing philosophy."

"How long have you been here?"

"Oh, about ten minutes. Where were you?"

"I had to go to the store to get some stuff for the dinner. I hope you like Chinese food."

"I love Chinese food. The hotter the better." Kirchner's Woman's Roommate had moved off the couch and into the kitchen. Kirchner's Woman put the bag of groceries down and sat down next to me on the couch. She took a sip of my beer.

"Are you hungry?"

"Yes, very. I brought some wine."

"That's okay, I got some saki. It's the cheap stuff, but I love it." Kirchner's Woman's Roommate came back into the room.

"I have to go to the library to study, so I guess I'll see you guys later. It was very nice talking to you."

"It was very nice talking to you."

"Maybe I'll see you around."

"Probably."

"Bye."

"Bye."

"Goodbye. I'll leave the door unlocked," Kirchner's Woman said.

JOIN THE PARTY!

The Party Line: A Great New Way To Meet Men and Women

The Party Line is a fun new way to meet people - without ever leaving your home or office! One call puts you in the middle of an ongoing conversation with a lively group of men and women. A cross-section of city-dwellers, eager to talk, and perhaps meet. Our exciting conference call is fun and safe.

Our popular Party Lines across the country have created a sensation. Now you can join the excitement. It's simple! Just dial 100-433-799-555-8888-3333 from any phone and you'll find yourself meeting people right away.

No credit cards, no pre-payment, no extra bills to pay. We've arranged for you to be discreetly billed on your telephone bill automatically. Dial 100-433-799-555-8888-3333 and get in on the fun today! It's much less expensive than a dating service, only $1 a minute. Stay on as long as you like.

Sometimes people let the same problem make them miserable for years when they could just say, "So what." That's one of my favorite things to say," So what."

"My mother didn't love me." So what.

"My husband won't ball me." So what.

"I'm a success but I'm still alone." So what.

I don't know how I made it through all the years before I learned how to do that trick. It took a long time for me to learn it, but once you do, you never forget.

Do you want me to drive for awhile I ask Sure if you don't mind we pull over to the side of the road we switch places I take the wheel So you two knew each other in Colorado was she married to Odets then They weren't married but they saw a great deal of each other that's how I met Frances you know through Odets Oh yeah Yeah when I first got here I needed a place to stay until I got myself together and Odets gave me Frances' phone number We're all one big happy family I say Well not that happy

Frances wasn't exactly pleased that I was friends with Kirchner's Woman she let me stay in her apartment but didn't exactly make me feel all that welcome it was only later when I had a big falling out with Kirchner's Woman that Frances and I became friends.

A boy grabs her hair and drags her outside the building into an alley. She refuses to look at him he hits her in the face with his fist. Her mouth opens but no sound escapes it's like television with the sound off. He's beating her now coolly efficiently silently expertly. Her reactions are perfectly synchronized with his actions it all seems choreographed. She's fallen he's kicking her in the face and stomach still no sound. Smashed nose split lips shattered cheek bright purple and red he takes out a knife reaches down carefully takes a slice out of her right earlobe puts it in his pocket her face seems to melt into the asphalt he brushes past me I notice how colorful her face is against the dark blue of the alley. I go to Frances to try to stop the bleeding.

I'm totally positive about the yuppies. What do they want? They want money? Well, who doesn't? People say yuppies are apathetic. I say that's crazy. You can't be apathetic. . . to be a yuppie, you have to chose the food at the gourmet deli, what kind of arugula you're going to get. . . . I mean it's hard work to get up and diet and plan your life. . . .

Changing the world is not done in a day. And I think that what most of us learned in the sixties was that you've got to get your own act together, and if you can't chose lettuce with confidence, and if you can't pick your BMW, how can you pick a government?

One morning we awaken with my hands around your throat.

I'm tired of talking I'm tired of driving I'm tired of everything I turn and look at Sally she's staring out the window a peaceful look on her face I wonder what she's thinking I consider asking her but instead I turn the radio up louder and smile I realize my inefficacy but that knowledge doesn't really help.

"Why don't you set the table. Here's some matches for the candles. The chopsticks are in the drawer next to the sink."
"Smells great."
"I hope you like it hot."
"I like it real hot."
"Sounds like it might turn out to be an exciting evening. Do you want another beer?"
"Isn't the saki warm yet?"
"Not quite. Why don't you put some music on."
"Sure, what would you like?"
"Some nice dinner music... something sensuous. Something that won't interrupt. I hate to be interrupted."
"Yeah, me too."

By Halloween I'd like to be off. I've got to detox myself from the V's with ativans - Ativan covers a V habit but don't give you seizures when you eventually stop taking them. When you get off all the pills, you can even feel your dose again. I'm so jealous of the people who are on 35 or below - they get Dolophine in their juice. Dolophine comes in pills and it takes the nurse longer to crush it up. It's cleaner and I hear you feel it more intensely. I don't think it would be a bad thing if I stayed on juice a little longer. It would be good if I even got off by Thanksgiving, but if I have to I'll stay on until early next year.

"Of all melancholy topics, what, according to the universal understanding of mankind, is the most melancholy?" death - was the obvious reply. "And when," I said, "is this most melancholy of topics most poetical?" From what I have already explained at some length, the answer, here also, is obvious - "When it most closely allies itself to Beauty: the death, then, of a beautiful woman is, unquestionably, the most poetical topic in the world."

Sally Raoul Sweet Jane Joe Toulouse-Lautrec and I all drive up in Sally's car to visit Frances at the sanitarium where her mother had her committed about six months ago today's the first day she's been allowed to have visitors so we're all very excited Raoul and Toulouse-Lautrec and of course Sally have all visited mental hospitals before but all hospitals give Sweet Jane the creeps especially mind joints she says so she's a bit hesitant but the rest of us are joyous and full of hope undaunted by the small brown stone structures squatting around a central courtyard all surrounded by a large grass field with lots of trees a rather peaceful place one had to admit we walk up to the front desk of the center building and ask the nurse on duty where Frances Farmer is she gives us a little map and points to one of the small buildings set off a bit from the main square and tells us that if we get lost to ask someone where Heaven is we laugh at that then Toulouse-Lautrec says that used to be the nickname of San Francisco too we laugh louder at that walk out the door in search of Heaven.

ARTFORUM

Toulouse-Lautrec - Bank of America Gallery, San Francisco

Toulouse-Lautrec has spent much time over the years in the houses of prostitution, even living for awhile in one of the more fashionable houses in San Francisco's North Beach area. Thus he has become familiar with every aspect of the daily routine there and was able to make paintings of the girls performing their toilet, or making their beds, or just watching tv in an off moment. Some of these paintings are on exhibit in the current Bank of America

Gallery show in San Francisco.

Among these paintings are some glimpses into the more intimate life of the girls, as for example in a picture called "Tender Loins," where women are shown parading for the medical inspection to which they willingly submit themselves at regular intervals. In spite of its unpleasing subject and the possibilities of indulging in salaciousness, Lautrec had made a picture which is neither pornographic nor erotic.

There is a remarkable lack of primness or shame in the postures and expressions of these two girls, who are subtly characterized, nor has Lautrec tried to disguise their indifference by introducing a note of *espielgerie* in the manner of a Wesselmann or Mel Ramos. The inspection is merely a part of the boring routine of their everyday lives and they are presenting themselves un-self-consciously. One of the most remarkable characteristics of Lautrec's work is that he is able to see and record impartially.

I think Elvis Presley is the first protestant saint.

All my life I didn't want it to be only words. I went on living just because I didn't want it so. Now, too, I want it every day not to be words.

We walk around the green grass yards for awhile looking for Heaven Raoul has the map so we let him be leader we see a group of patients in wheelchairs sunning themselves another group is playing croquet on the lawn still another group sits playing cards on a red picnic table this place seems luxurious almost like a resort the doctors guards nurses and attendants are not dressed in any sort of uniform they are hard to distinguish from the patients maybe they walk a bit more upright or perhaps they are a bit more aware of the other human beings they come into contact with but these are just guesses the truth of the matter is we really can't tell the difference between the patients and the staff soon we are playing a game called guess the patients some are easy most of the ones playing croquet probably are patients and the ones wandering around alone at the edge of the grass yard and of course the ones in wheelchairs but many are more difficult the fellow in the ivory suit watching the croquet players or the woman walking quickly past us and up the stairs into one of the small brown buildings and a group of men having snacks on the lawn next to a fountain Toulouse breaks off from the group and walks over to speak to those men.

How Each Of Us Is Most Afraid of Dying

Sally —Being raped and strangled by a serial killer.

Joe—Being an innocent bystander and getting shot in a drug or gang war.

Sweet Jane—Dying of AIDS.

Toulouse-Lautrec—Being poisoned, either purposely or accidentally.

Frances Farmer—Committing suicide by overdosing with sleeping pills.

La Galoue—Being a bag lady and dying of hunger or exposure.

Art—Getting electrocuted or being struck by lightning.

Sue Side—Refuses to think about death.

Raoul—Is afraid of getting run over by a Yugo or a Hyundai or a really cheap Ford.

Me—I'm afraid of dying of cancer, or a heart attack.

Rapist is Defiant on Eve of Return to Society

Convicted of raping a young girl, hacking off her arms and leaving her for dead, Lawrence Singleton was given the maximum sentence - 14 years.

At 12:01 Monday, Singleton, 60, becomes a free man - his parole terminated - and with a series of unexpectedly defiant statements, he has assured for himself a return to society fitting his notoriety.

Breaking a self-imposed silence to claim again that he was innocent, Singleton two weeks ago threatened to sue Mary Vincent, the girl he kidnapped, raped and mutilated in September 1978. He accused her of inflicting emotional distress on him.

Ms. Vincent immediately ordered her lawyer to seek enforcement of the $2.5 million judgement that was awarded her in Nevada last year. She previously had made no attempt to collect.

Singleton was convicted in 1979 of picking up hitchhiker Vincent in Berkeley to take her to Interstate 5, about 50 miles east. Instead her drove to rural Stanislaus County, raped her repeatedly, hacked off her arms with an ax and left her to die in a culvert.

Ms. Vincent crawled out and was found by a passing motorist.

Thomas Smith Jr., pastor of the Bride of Christ Church in Azeal Ore., earlier this month invited Singleton to live and work on the church compound. Singleton said he would either go to Oregon or Florida.

Ah wassa born . . . .

+ Lord shakin', even then was dumpt into some icy font, like some great stinky unclean,

From slum-church to slum-church split mah heart to some fat cunt behind a screen. . . E-eeevil poppin eye pressed up to the opening, He'd slide shut the lil perforated hatch. . . at night my body blushed to the whistle of the birch. . .with a lil practice I soon learned to use it on mahself. . . Punishment?! Reward!! Punishment?! Reward!!

Well, ah tied on. . . percht on mah bed, ah was. . . sticken a needle in mah arm. . . Ah tied off! Fucken wings burst on mah back (like ah was cuttin teeth).

Lautrec quickly rejoins the group What did you say to them I asked them how to get to Heaven And what did they say They told me to believe in God and pray Really No that's a little joke they told me to walk down past that building and turn to the right What else did they say They asked who I was looking for and I told them and then they shook their heads said Heaven is a pretty rough place Then what did they say Nothing then they started eating again Do you think they're patients or staff Lautrec shrugs his shoulders I have no idea he says anyway what difference does it make.

"This is really good."
"I'm glad you like it."
"Would you like some more saki?"
"I'd love some."

REJECTED

Surrogate mother Patty Nowkowski of Detroit, Mich., and her husband, Aaron, welcome home 2-week-old Arthur Jay from the hospital after the woman gave birth to twins. Nowkowski says the couple who hired her as a surrogate decided they did not want the boy but only wanted to keep the girl.

The evil and the good know themselves only by giving up their secret face to face. The true good who meets the true evil (Holy Mother of Mercy! are there any such?) learns for the first time how to accept neither; the face of the one tells the face of the other the half of the story that both forgot.

We all walk a little bit faster now our exuberance has worn off we want to see Frances as soon as possible this is no game we hurry past the building in front of us then turn to our right we stop abruptly in front of us looms a large grey building much newer than the rest it doesn't look like a resort at all it looks like a huge postmodern torture chamber grey concrete walls windows so tiny bars are unnecessary Sweet Jane turns away we all shudder Toulouse says I spent some time in an asylum once in France it was not so bad something like the Betty Ford clinic in the United States it was very expensive and very discrete my parents paid for it Raoul pushes a doorbell on the side of the door a voice responds immediately asks us who we wish to see Raoul shouts Frances Farmer the door opens electronically a large woman at a small grey desk points to some chairs and tells us someone will be with us directly it's very cool inside the building the room smells slightly of antiseptic we all sit in the chairs without saying a word.

I'm sitting here alone and quiet and someone comes for me. There are two of them they call my name tell me to get up and follow them I do they remind me of some people I used to know I can't remember who. I wonder if we are going to the drug room or the big cold bathtub and I hesitate in the hallway but then one of them tells me to hurry up my friends are waiting for me. Waiting for me waiting to see me I wonder how I look is my hair okay I wish I had put on another dress instead of this old pale green one pale green like the halls of the drug room pale green like some of my snot I wipe on my pillow case. Our art seems in the last few years to be leaving its experimental period behind. Suddenly almost too suddenly like those quick cuts you see in the movies I don't want to see them I mean I don't want them to see me. To see me like this. This isn't me this isn't how I really am. I feel like I've been appropriated stolen desecrated like that guy who painted a moustache on the Mona Lisa. What was his name? I don't want my friends to laugh at me. What will my friends think of me when they see me like this? What will I say to them what will I tell them? I wonder what they will ask me.

I stop walking. I don't want to see them. I want to go back to the big room and hide under the covers of my bed. I want to lie there and think about the movies I used to make. One of the guards turns around and says What's the matter Frances don't you want to see your friends? He wants to fuck me I know he does. He probably already has. I want to puke. I want to puke puke green all over my pale green dress. I want to puke puke green all over the guard's stupid fucking fat yellow face. How to Buy A Performance. Instead of puking I ask the other guard how I look. C'mon Frances you look fine. One of the guards I'm not sure if it's the one I hate or the other one it doesn't make any difference I hate them both touches me lightly on the elbow and gets me walking again. I walk with him partly because I'm surprised at his light touch.

What will I say? Will I tell them about how the minute I open my eyes in the morning I immediately want to throw up? And when I go down to breakfast in the bright blue and yellow room I can't stand to even put one bite in my mouth and I say to myself O my God here it comes again. Big name artists like Salle and Schnabel will both probably clear $1 million this year. And then when Doctor Pusface asks me if I ate breakfast that day I tell him yes and he writes something in his little book and says Frances you're making tremendous progress and then he sends me to the puke green pill room and I take two bright pink pills and one white capsule and I drink the orange juice like I'm supposed to and then I go to the bathroom and look in the mirror to see who I am. And I never can tell.

There they are. Whereof one cannot speak thereof one must be silent. They are so glad to see me they say. I look great they say it looks like I've been getting some sun they say. How's the food here they ask. They spoke to my mother and she says that I'll probably be released in a couple of months they say. One of the guards says that we can go into one of the conference rooms so we all walk single file down an orange hall until we reach a pale blue room with sky blue chairs and deep blue carpeting I notice that in this room even the kleenex is blue. I've never been here before in this blue room.

We all sit down in the large blue chairs. I'm still trying to think of something to say. I don't want to talk about me it makes no sense to talk about me. What is me? John Lennon Shot To Death Outside Home. It's not like I don't exist it's more like I exist everywhere I'm too many to pin down. This doesn't feel particularly good it makes me dizzy to think about it. If You Drive Don't Drink If You Drink Don't Drive.

I have to say something. Sometimes it seems like such a far distance between my brain and my mouth that I have to start speaking in my brain minutes before anything comes out of my mouth. How was the drive? I hear myself say. My voice sounds weak and far away I sound like a very sick person. They all answer at once. The drive was fine this is a nice place very pretty and shady we saw a deer on the way up they say. I nod and pretend to listen. I think back to when one of the male nurses raped me in the silver stainless steel bathtub the lights were too bright they hurt my eyes he was small and hairy I thought at first he was going to drown me when I found out all he wanted to do was rape me I was somewhat relieved. It was over quickly and afterwards he was almost nice about it he rubbed my shoulders and gave me a pack of cigarettes and then he left me alone to soak it's the only time I've been really alone in this fucking place. I turned the whirlpool on and pretended I was in my bathtub at home.

The Bill Blass show was so fabulous in its own way that you practically had to be there to get it. Another pregnant pause another awkward silence why are they all staring at me haven't they ever seen a sick person before? Someone needs to say something why should it be me please someone say something for Christ's sake. Rogue Priest Suspected in IRA Killings. I wonder how I look to them now. I wonder if I look a lot different I wonder if I have that vacant crazy expression on my face I wonder if that's the reason they all keep staring intently at me. I have nothing to tell them why don't they say something.

Actually I do have something to tell them a secret my secret is that I have no secrets I have no depth just an infinite number of surfaces if they could strip away one mask they would only see another that's what I try to tell the doctors but the doctors just smile and say that I'm making wonderful progress two ships that pass each other in the night should always buy each other break-fast the doctors are still looking for my secrets the guards when they rape me are looking for my secrets even the other patients when they make fun of me cut my hair and put lipstick all over my face and spit on me and tease me they too are looking for my secrets the judge was looking for my secrets but I showed him called him a cocksucker it breaks your new dreams daily h-block long kesh that shut him up but even my mother yes even my own mother is looking for my secrets that's why she put me in here to find my little Frances Farmer secrets but I've fooled them I've sold all my secrets traded them all for cigarettes or books or little sticks of lipstick all except one I've only got one secret left and that's that I have no secrets this way I can laugh at anything I'll be damned if I'll give this secret up why don't they say something why do they sit here in this powder blue room and just stare at me what can I say to them there's no me no me no me I'm too sick for parody ban roll-on keeps on working there's no me that's why I've never tried to kill myself what would be the point a thousand stainless steel surfaces glittering in the sun a million tiny pools of water with no depth a trillion flecks of radioactive confetti all with no origin and no direction that's what I really look like not this ugly girl in the puke green dress sitting in the middle of a powder blue room I could just doze off right here this chair is very soft and warm I could just float away on this chair float up toward the ceiling fly though the sky blue ceiling float up toward the sun like that greek guy like my dreams when I was a kid and I remember when I flew to the soviet union that time it was like I was floating on a cloud that would be fun to just float away kill kill kill kill kill the poor and see my friends their mouths gaping o frances you can float they would say I'm not really sure who these people are the guard said they are my friends but I'm not so sure maybe my mother sent them to spy on me it wouldn't matter it wouldn't bother me nothing bothers me because there is no me I can laugh at anything it's got a new motorola microprocessor with 2 megabytes ram and 35 meg hard disk with mouse and full tech support I can laugh at anything that's one good thing about being sick you can laugh and nobody asks you why when my friend Robin died I laughed all day and all night it felt like I was laughing for weeks they had to give me a pill to make me go to sleep and then I laughed in my dreams why don't these people say something to me I think I'll laugh at them right in their faces the laugh of a very sick woman they won't get mad they'll only feel sorry for me then when they leave they'll shake their heads and say she's worse than we thought maybe she won't be released as soon as we expected I'm tired I'm tired of this blue room with this blue carpet chairs walls and kleenex I'm tired of these silent faces I don't want to look at them anymore I want to go back to my bed and go to sleep why don't they say anything wait now I understand maybe they're just like me maybe they're sick like me maybe they have scars on their wits I mean wrists like me maybe they only have one secret just like me maybe we share this secret maybe the whole world shares this secret that there are no secrets that's a very pretty dress you have on Frances

why are they whispering why are they talking so low why don't they speak louder they did say something to me I need to answer my mouth and tongue are so far away it will take such a long time to answer I need to say something to them why did they do this to me what do they want from me I need to say something I know I need to say something I'm sorry I say fuck fuck fuck that wasn't right that wasn't right at all what did they say to me I forgot I need to say something else I don't know why I'm having so much trouble today maybe it's the pills god damn it god damn it okay okay okay okay I chose an eternity of this I need to think I need to just stop and think one of my friends they're not my friends Robin was my friend and now she's dead one of the women walks up to me don't touch me don't you dare touch me get away get away it's all right Frances it's all right she says

her voice is nice she reaches out to touch me I draw back I notice that there's dark red blood on my hand how did it get there it's all right she says it's all right I like the way her voice sounds maybe she's right maybe it is all right she moves her hand toward mine I let her touch me her hand is cold but that's all right I wonder where that blood came from I feel I should say something to her maybe if I say something she'll talk to me in that nice voice of hers Amaretto di

Janowitz she starts to smooth my hair with her hand I know I need to say something thank you there I think that was right it feels nice her hand smoothing my hair I want to tell this woman about my friend Robin about how she died right after I took that electricity in my head I start to tell her but all that comes out of my mouth is it's very hard to be just one person she smiles at that she says it's impossible I remember kissing a man under the covers of a dark bed it was very cold in the room even colder outside if you kept your head above the covers you could see your breath I don't know why I thought of that just now I'm not really sure if it was a movie I was in or not I guess it really doesn't make much difference sometimes I get confused I'm not sure if what I remember really happened to me or not I guess that's not so crazy I remember after Robin died and before I started laughing someone poured me a cup of coffee and I put some milk in it to cool it down because the coffee was too hot and it burned my tongue when I tried to take a sip I remember the way that the white milk swirled around in the coffee I didn't stir it I just watched it swirl around the crystal escalator in the palace of god department store and then I put some more milk in it and it became lighter and lighter and I put the cup in my hand and swirled it around until finally it was just that one color that light brown and I don't like that color at all so I put some more milk in it and some of the milk spilled over the side of the cup and in my lap and then someone yelled at me and I had to go back to my bed that was when I decided that I didn't want any secrets any more you have such beautiful hair I always wanted to have hair like yours she has such a sweet voice not like those doctors especially that new one I call him Doctor Gucci he thinks he's so smart he's the one that puts the electricity in my head covert actions traced to white house afterwards sometimes I can't walk and I pee on myself that's when I found out who I really was after the electricity and after Robin died after I went in my bed with the milk still dripping from my dress that's when I knew they couldn't hurt me because there was no me to hurt and so I started laughing and I haven't stopped I'm laughing now I'm laughing as this woman strokes my hair it feels so nice look Frances we brought you some things

one of the men moves closer to me he's awful short maybe he's walking on his knees to fool me he holds out a paper bag he holds it open I look up at the woman stroking my hair she nods slowly I don't know why invention it must be humbly admitted does not consist in creating out of a void but out of chaos I don't know what I'm supposed to do why are they all watching me why do they stare at me so don't they know that I'm not well why do they force me to react to them why can't I just laugh and be left alone I look up at the sky ceiling wonder if the ceiling is a way out go on Frances take it I hear the nice voice say I need to do something I need to say something I have to go to the bathroom I say I have to go to the bathroom I can see each individual word come out of my mouth and float slowly up to the ceiling like bubbles or clear balloons this is wonderful it's kind of like a cartoon or something the words just drift out of my mouth up to the ceiling I want to see more words I have to pee I say and the words just come out one right after the other its like I'm back in the old house on fenton street and my mom's reading the paper and I'm blowing soap bubbles in the sun my words float up until they reach the ceiling then they burst into a million pieces and these pieces float down on us like warm snow at mcdonald's it's mac tonight our father who art in heaven I say and the words spew out of my mouth and waft slowly up to the ceiling and I look up to the ceiling and the word pee has just burst into a million tiny pieces of pure light and these pieces float down slowly like snow like warm wonderful snow and I want to fill up the whole room with this snow what are you looking at Frances they can't see the snow hallowed be thy name thy kingdom come thy will be done I can't remember the rest and the words are just floating up to the ceiling crowding and bumping into each other gently my name is Frances Farmer I live at 2121 fenton street seattle washington united states of america planet earth milky way and the bubbles of words are thick now and the word-snow is falling down thickly covering up this blue carpet was it zsa zsa or eva gabor who co-starred in green acres covering up the blue chairs and the tables and the faces and heads of these people dulling the outlines softening the shapes it's getting hard to think of any more words what was that song Robin and I used to sing I can't remember it was a song she really liked we used to sing it and then she'd call me her little flower I'm the bird and you're my little flower and then she would tell me stories and we'd giggle and smoke cigarettes and drink coke I remember seeing the two orange tips of our cigarettes in the dark blackness and thinking sad thoughts the nurses would get so mad at me and they'd scold me and tell me if I wouldn't go to sleep they'd give me something to knock me out but we didn't care we didn't care at all she was my little bird and I was her little flower why can't I remember that song my words have all popped now the snow is almost gone the outlines of the chairs and tables and things are becoming more distinct everything's becoming too clear I need more words it was the night before christmas and all through the house not a creature was stirring not even a mouse something's wrong we'd better call a nurse something's wrong we'd better call a nurse I repeat and the words float upward and the snow starts again and I say anything that comes into my head I have a friend named Robin and we used to drink soda and sing this song together but I can't remember the song and I can't remember what Robin looks like she did have a real nice voice I was mean to her once and I bit her but she forgave she really did she said she loved all my movies and all around the words float up and pop pop pop and the snow falls down and covers everything blue with this warm whitenes and the snow from my words is so thick that all I can see are vague outlines and blurry shapes and someone asks me are you okay and this time I know what to say and I can't see anything but I know what to say I say I'm fine I'm fine no really everything is fine.

Frances is getting out and we're having a surprise party for her at this fresh Berkeley hot spot *The New Historicism* Lautrec has rented it out and we're all here being seen even Kirchner's Woman is coming back from New York actually Frances has already been released into the custody of her mother and her mother is going to keep her in isolation she's not going to let her read listen to music or watch tv thinks that this might be the only way to save Frances we're videotaping this party and we'll send her one of the tapes hopefully her mother will let her watch it we're also going to call her at her mother's house and yell surprise it should be fun it's a costume party the theme is come as your favorite literary personality of romanticism I'm looking forward to seeing Kirchner's Woman again.

When Joe gets horny and can't get a woman he can: polish the bayonet, lope the mule, bop the baloney, choke the chicken, fight the cat, clap with one hand, buff the helmet, grease the pig, stroke the salami, milk the cow, tickle the pickle, bang the drum, saddle the steed, climb the rope, pull the taffy, cream the coffee, launch the missile, finger the dinger, ying the yang, feed the sheets, pinch the inch, skin the snake, walk the dog, frig the frog, fidget with the digit, count to eleven, visit Lady Hand, see Rosy Palm and her five sisters, oil his shorts, pull the pud, slap the monkey etc.. When Sally gets horny and can't get a man, all she can do is masturbate.

Reflections on Rita
She knows an eleven letter word for 'senator.'
Reads the last page of a good book first.
And her legs? Don't get me started.

We enjoy indulging ourselves in the logic that kills.

I have a hard time deciding between Percy Bysshe and Mary Wollstonecraft finally I choose Percy Bysshe Sally helps make me up we make my face all white and bloated and I glue a few small rubber fish to my face the triumph of life Sally wearing a blue and white sheet with white paper-mache peaks on her shoulders and one on her head she's the alps her head-peak is hard to drink from she has to use a straw I wonder how long she'll wear it Raoul is a clubfooted Lord Byron Sweet Jane is dressed in a white birdsuit Joe is dressed like a movie Frankenstein Lautrec and La Galoue are Keats and Psyche respectively even Kirchner's Woman's Roommate is here dressed as Absolute Knowledge or something Art and Sue haven't arrived yet neither has Kirchner's Woman Raoul hands me a glass filled with green liquid laudanum my boy he asks I sniff the glass wonder if he's kidding or not.

Match the alcohol drug combination with the appropriate character:
A) Moet Brut and quaaludes
B) Cuervo Gold and peyote
C) Laphroag Unblended Single Malt and Black Beauties
D) Guinness Stout and crystal meth
E) Pharmaceutical coke and Bombay and tonic
F) Ecstacy and saki
G) Pernod and opium
H) Methadone and Bailey's Irish Cream
I) Thai Stick and Courvoissier
J) Crack and Chartreuse

1) Sweet Jane
2) Frances Farmer
3) Sally
4) Raoul
5) Art
6) Sue Side
7) La Galoue
8) Joe
9) Toulouse-Lautrec
10) the narrator

Gang Members Beat Man,
Rape Wife While Crowd Watches

San Francisco- A San Francisco resident was severely beaten and forced to watch while his wife was repeatedly raped on the El Cerrito BART platform late last night. A gang of six or seven so-called "skinheads" reportedly were harassing an elderly black woman when Michael Downly, 29, objected to their racial slurs. The youths confronted Downly, and soon began to strike and beat him about the face and head. His wife, Marcia, age 26, ran to a phone and attempted to call the police, but was caught and dragged to the edge of the platform, where she was reportedly raped six or seven times until police arrived. Police confirmed reports that there were at least seven or eight bystanders who refused to come to the aid of the Downlys.

Even with the arrival of these samplers, sampling is nothing new. Turntables have always been used in hip-hop as a form of sampler, and one cannot look at popular American music—of which America is the casing, Europe the fuse, and Africa the gun powder—without realizing that it is all "samples" from other sources. I mean, Elvis launched a career and sold a billion records by spit-shining r&b jams and "sampling" African-American song and dance styles. Gospel lyrics consist almost entirely of "sampled" writ, reworked bits and pieces of Bible text. The difference is that the King James Version is in the public domain, as are, unfortunately, African-American song and dance styles. James Brown's "Funky Drummer," Bob James's "Take Me to the Mardi Gras" and now, Elvis's cover of "Tutti Frutti" are all registered with the U.S. Copyright Office.

I walk over to Absolute Knowledge she's with this guy dressed as Kubla Khan they both have glasses of champagne in their hands How are you I ask I'm a little bit drunk she answers who are you I'm Percy Bysshe Shelley I answer No who are you in real life I'm a friend of your former roommate I came over for dinner once Oh yeah that's right you're the comedian Yeah that's right how's philosophy coming along any new breakthroughs that I should hear about I suppose that you've heard that God doesn't exist Yeah a long time ago Well now they think that He might He might what He might exist Are you kidding me Would Absolute Knowledge kid you I don't know say since you're absolute and everything do you know when she's coming When who's coming Your roommate My former roommate Yeah your former roommate do you know when she's coming Yes I do When I can't tell you just because I'm absolute doesn't mean I'm easy.

"Watch out for those red dragons," she warned me.

"Yeah, I see them. This is really terrific, what all do you put into it?" I asked as I chased a piece of shrimp down with my chopsticks.

"Lot's of stuff; shrimp, rice, soy sauce, ginger, other spices. I'm glad you like it." She poured more saki into my tiny porcelain cup.

"Sure. Now I know why you have to sit on the floor at those Japanese restaurants, so you can just slide down and sleep after the saki. This is really powerful stuff."

"I really like it. I drink it with everything. Even though the dinner is Chinese instead of Japanese, I think it fits." She looked into my eyes. "It makes me really horny," she said.

"Yeah, me too."
"Have you ever been tied up?" she asked me.

Next on Donahue - Men who have sex changes and the women who love them.

There were not always novels in the past, and there will not always have to be; not always tragedies, not always great epics; not always were the forms of commentary, translation, indeed, even so-called plagiarism, playthings in the margins of literature; they had a place not only in the philosophical but also in the literary writings of Arabia and China. All this to accustom you to the thought that we are in the midst of a mighty recasting of literary forms, a melting down in which many of the opposites in which we have been used to think may lose their force.

Everyone here is much too clever for words here I see Art and Sue Side come up the staircase Kirchner's Woman is not with them Art is dressed like Friedrich Schlegel and Sue is Dorothea Hi Art hi Sue how's it going How are you says Art rather stiffly Pretty good pretty good that's a nice costume you've got on there Thank you says Art have you see Lautrec I have to speak with him immediately Yeah he's over there by the bar Thank you Art and Sue scurry away What the fuck's wrong with them I need a drink I turn and look for Absolute Knowledge or the alps.

Joe's clock broke the other day and he was sure it was Sunday but it was really only Saturday. He went out and bought the paper and he couldn't find the comics or the recipes or anything else of the Sunday paper features and he was so angry that he went back to the store and asked them where the rest of his paper was. They laughed at him and told him it was Saturday not Sunday. Joe's flat was broken into the other day. They didn't take anything except his clothes. Now everyone Joe sees looks like they're wearing his clothes.

A new book, called *Kitchen Spanish*, is designed to permit wealthy people to communicate with their Spanish-speaking domestic staff. The book consists entirely of direct orders in Spanish, with their English translations.

Entertainment through pain.

I walk over to the alps What's up I ask The sky she answers That's great I say really fucking terrific you should be on Carson What's with you she asks Why don't you take your peak off and let me see your face for a change You've seen my face plenty of times why is tonight so special One mask after another isn't it Why are you being such a jerk tonight relax have a drink I'm sure she'll show You're not being very sympathetic tonight are you Fuck you I'm tired of being your big sister you want to cry cry on somebody else's shoulder tonight I just want to see your face while I talk to you that's all Well tonight that's asking too much See ya later Sally Yeah see ya later there's a lot of tension in the air tonight I don't know why.

Sweet Jane was walking home alone after rehearsing with the band on Sunday night. She was in a tight blue funk, really depressed. Sundays always got to her as it was, and this Sunday she was really broke, had only a five dollar bill until the next Tuesday. She was sick of everybody: she felt envious of those who had more money than she did, and she felt tired of those who had less. She tried to put out these 'leave-me-the-fuck-alone' vibes so she wouldn't get panhandled, but this old bum came up to her anyway trying to spare-change her, and she lost her cool and started yelling at him. "Who in the holy fuck do you think you are, you cocksucking pus-filled leech. Do I look like some fucking rich saint to you, you stupid dirtball scumbag. Look at these fucking clothes, you blind old goat, look at these fucking rags. You should be giving me money, you greasy jerk." A few people stopped and watched, and the old man slunk away, and Sweet Jane felt totally ashamed of herself. She promised to give her five dollars away to the next person who asked for money, but nobody else approached her that night.

Excuses, they don't mean anything to your thighs, okay? Excuses are not going to lift up your butt.

The really central insight of Christianity is sin.

I leave the alps and walk up to Byron Frankenstein Psyche and The Albatross may I join you I ask Why are we falling apart asks Sweet Jane Jesus I don't know if I can take much more of this I order a glass of champagne mixed with cognac Don't we ever get tired of this I ask Byron don't we ever get sick of being so clever and so ironic Sure we do says Byron sure we do.

"Why don't we sit on the couch?"
"Is there any dessert?" I asked.
She smiled. "Perhaps later. Do you like Eno?"
"Yes, as a matter of fact, I do." She set two lighted candles on the coffee table in front of me, changed the tape, and then turned out the lights and sat down next to me. She threw her head back and smiled. "That was a great dinner," I said.
"Thank you very much."
"You're very welcome."
"Are you trying to seduce me?"
"I haven't heard that word in a long time. Yes, I guess you could say that I'm trying to seduce you."
"Well, it's working." I leaned over to her and we began to kiss.

Triple Treat—Two girls and one guy sample each other in every conceivable way.
Here's Looking at You—Kerri Foxx looks directly at you, while doing it!

Dark and Sweet—Black guy and sweet blonde girls.
Girls Who Love It—The title says it all!
Endless Orgies—Dozens of orgies fill this tape.
Voyeur's Dream—Six hunks going at it alone (all male).
Dildo Girls—You can probably guess what this one's all about.
Kiss and Swell—The ultimate oral orgy.
Foreskin Foreplay—An anthology of the biggest and the best (all male).
Anything Goes—Three girls in search of the ultimate orgasm.

Sherrie Levine has decided simply to represent the idea of creativity, re-presenting someone else's work as her own in an attempt to sabotage a system that places value on the privileged production of individual talent. She articulates the realization that, given a certain set of constraints, those imposed by an understanding of the current situation as much as those imposed by a desire to appear "correct" in a theoretical and political sense, there is nothing to be done, that creative activity is rendered impossible. And so, like any dispossessed victim she simply steals what she needs. Levine's appropriations are the underside of Schnabel's misappropriations, and the two find themselves in a perverse lockstep. The extremity of her position doubles back on her, infecting her work with an almost romantic poignancy as resistant to interpretation as the frank romanticism of her nemesis.

Don't we ever get tired of this I repeat don't we ever get tired of going with the flow following the flux What do you suggest Lord Byron asks I don't know some depth some change at least some break in the rhythm You want punctuation The Albatross says Something like that yeah I want my life to mean something is that too much to ask Keats comes by with his video camera Schlegel is holding a light tree Lautrec says nothing just shoots I hold up my glass salute the camera Byron holds up his clubfoot

Sweet Jane flaps her wings Psyche does a little twirl Frankenstein growls then says Come on everyone let's say something to Frances we all line up like a portrait around one of the tables we hold our glasses up and say We love you Frances we love you come back soon we clink our glasses together and drink our drinks That was nice Lautrec says that was very nice.

Sally, Sweet Jane and La Galoue are drinking margaritas at the *Asja Lacis*. It's late, they're not the only ones left but pretty close. Sweet Jane has just asked Sally when she first saw a penis.

"I'm really not sure if this is a dream or not, but I seem to remember being four or five years old, and I was at my grandmother's house for a big family reunion. There was this young boy, maybe five or six, and he wasn't part of our family or anything, he wasn't one of my cousins or anything like that.

Anyway, we went into the bathroom and he showed me his and I showed him mine, and I remember him calling his a peanut, and I also remember that we couldn't think of an adequate word for mine, for my 'thing' you know. It was funny, but even then I thought that the word peanut wasn't very impressive, but it was still better than nothing, than calling it a 'thing' or a hole.'"

Have You Seen Me?
Name: Bobby Dunn
Age: 12
Last Seen: Walking home from school in Louisville, Kentucky, on October 12, 1984
Background: Bobby was last seen wearing a brown and white windbreaker, a solid white tee-shirt, and blue-denim jeans. His father and mother were divorced in 1982, custody was granted to the mother. His father, Walter Dunn, has not been seen since the boy disappeared. Bobby likes basketball, art and computers. If you have seen Bobby, or any one of the thousands of lost or missing children, please call the CHILDREN'S HOTLINE, at 1-800-OUR-KIDS. The call is toll-free and confidential.

Give me new noise
Give me new affection
Strange new toys
From another land
I need to see more
Than three dimensions
Stranger than fiction
Faster than light

So you want meaning says Lord Byron you want some depth some soul I'm just tired of irony I say I'm just tired of all this surfaceness and shallowness I guess I want some continuity some sense of movement or experience I'm tired of all this decentering it's making me dizzy Perhaps you need a love says Psyche Don't we all says Frankenstein Love creates just as many problems as it solves says the Albatross Yeah but at least it's a different set of problems says Frankenstein If you aren't happy with yourself what makes you think you'll be happy with someone else says Byron I've heard all this before it's like we're rehearsing a scene from a movie and we're doomed to repetition until we get it right I guess I'm just bored I say maybe that's all it is just boredom Didn't Wilde say something about when a man thinks he has exhausted life it's usually the other way around says Byron I sip my drink and wonder when Kirchner's Woman is going to arrive.

All of a sudden we heard the door opening and then the lights flicking on. We both pulled away and then blinked at each other as Kirchner's Woman's Roommate walked in with an armful of books. She surveyed the scene and said "Oh, I'm so sorry for disturbing you, but I called and found out I don't have to work tonight, so I got a ride home from Karen. I won't bother you at all, I'm just going to go in my room and read."

"You're not bothering us at all," I said, as a brief but wicked thought flashed through my mind. Kirchner's Woman took her

hand from mine and drunk a tiny sip of saki.
"Do you want the lights on or off?"
Kirchner's Woman didn't answer. "Off," I said.
"I'm just going to fix myself a cup of tea, I'll only be a second.
Goodnight."
"Goodnight," I said. Kirchner's Woman got up off the couch
and walked into her bedroom. I followed.

Survey Lists 600,000 as Homeless
A new study by the Urban Institute concludes that the number
of homeless people in the United States is between 567,000 and
600,000.
That is far lower than estimates by some advocacy groups but
substantially higher than the 250,000 to 350,000 estimated in a
controversial report by the Department of Housing and Urban
development.
Martha Burt, co-author of the new study with Barbara Cohen,
said they conducted an extensive survey of more than 400 soup
kitchens and homeless shelters in the nation's largest cities with
major homeless problems to determine how many people used
them.
The survey found that most of the homeless eat 1.9 meals a day
and that more than a third reported that they regularly went
without food for at least one day a week.

The ownmost, non-relational possibility is not to be outstripped. Being toward this possibility enables Dasein to understand that giving itself up impends for it as the uttermost possibility of existence. Anticipation, however, unlike inauthentic Being-
towards-death, does not evade the fact that death is not to be
outstripped; instead, anticipation frees itself for accepting this.
When, by anticipation, one becomes free for one's own death, one
is liberated from one's lostness in these possibilities which may
accidentally thrust themselves upon one; and one is liberated in
such a way that for the first time one can authentically understand

and choose among the factical possibilities lying ahead of that possibility which is not to be outstripped. Anticipation discloses to existence that its uttermost possibility lies in giving itself up, and thus it shatters all one's tenaciousness to whatever existence one has reached.

Things used to be more fun it used to be more intense somehow more genuine don't you think and now it's just dull and grey Byron answers I don't think it was any worse or any better before it's always been pretty much the same That's exactly my point I say it's has always been pretty much the same with all our love for variety and newness we've grown accustomed to anything and now nothing makes a dent any more nothing really touches us You're a bit reactionary tonight says the Albatross maybe you need another drink You're right I do need another drink I say why do you think I'm being reactionary Just because you're without closure doesn't mean nobody else feels thinks or creates anything anymore just because you're not experiencing the comfort of significance doesn't mean that significance doesn't exist don't be so fucking naive it's not a mask that becomes you.

La Galoue has had four abortions. Sally has had two abortions. Kirchner's Woman has had one abortion. Sweet Jane has had two abortions. Sue Side has had five abortions.

STYLE, the image expressed by those comfortable with themselves. For many, personal style is creatively reflected by the body's closest environment - the clothing they wear.

At Tweeds, we have consistently admired the assured grace with which Europeans clothe themselves.

Equally, we continued to cherish the purely American qualities of ease and energy. And so we imagined a new kind of sportswear that blends the best of both - Casual American.

Our visions begin with a unified palette of rich colors and unexpected accents; colors that work together in surprisingly sophisticated ways. The collection is created from natural fibers that breathe and move with the body. Used in uncommon ways, they suggest a range of choices previously unavailable: classic clothes made from rayon and washed silk; adventurous pieces fashioned from familiar fabrics. Surprising, but for those who search for something different, ideal.

On these pages, you'll see clothes as versatile as the imaginations of those who wear them; shapes and colors that are accomplices in rule-breaking. They reveal the wearer's nature instead of concealing it. Pieces of clothing in which it's possible to feel comfortable in any situation. And we believe they're the only clothes worth having.

Thirty years old. There are no prizes.

I'm tired of talking You probably just need to get laid says Byron maybe we should have an orgy tonight I don't think that would help anyone says the Albatross Of course not I was just kidding one of the most interesting things about AIDS is that it has made the eros thanatos connection more explicit everyone knows now that fucking equals death Except this time it's no metaphor Well that's not so clear maybe it is and maybe it isn't anyway as I was saying maybe sex would do you good isn't that woman who you used to like coming tonight She was supposed to but I don't know what the deal with her husband is I don't think you have to worry about that says the Albatross Why I ask I'll tell you later she says.

"Close the door," she said. She had her back turned toward me, and I could see that she was unbuttoning the buttons of her blouse.

"Do you want the light on or off?"

"On. We should have brought those candles in from the living room." She turned around to face me. I could almost see the blush of her nipples in the folds of her unbuttoned blouse.

I'll go get them," I said, a bit hoarsely. She nodded. I turned, opened the door, and walked out to the living room. When I reached the candles on the coffee table I smiled to myself. I could feel my heart pounding. When I returned, she was lying underneath the covers, her blouse still hanging loosely from her shoulders. I slowly set the candles down on the night table next to the bed, and then sat on the bed to take my shoes off. She leaned over and lit the candles.

"Would you do me a big favor?"

"Sure, anything."

"Would you go and get the wine. I'm dying of thirst."

"Sure." I got up, went out of the bedroom and into the living room and then into the kitchen. I opened the refrigerator door and grabbed the bottle of wine. "Do we need glasses?"

"What?"

"I said do we need glasses?"

"Yes. The corkscrew is in the middle drawer, and the wine glasses are in the right cabinet over the sink." I opened the middle drawer, found the corkscrew, and then opened the cabinet door over the sink. Everything was right where she said it would be.

"Did you find them?"

"Yes." I returned to the bedroom, still smiling.

"You get undressed while I pour the wine." I leaned over to kiss her, then again sat on the bed and unbuttoned my shirt. I stood up and unbuttoned my pants just as the telephone rang. She looked at me apologetically. The phone rang again. She rolled over and picked up the receiver.

"Hello? Hi. I'm kind of busy right now, can I call you back tomorrow. I'm getting ready to go to sleep I know that listen I know that ok ok just a second alright." She put her hand over the receiver and turned to look at me. "I'm sorry, but I have to talk on the phone right now. I'll go out in the living room. Make yourself comfortable and I'll be back soon, I promise." She rose up on her knees and gave me a long, hard kiss. I put my hand gently on her left breast and caressed her nipple. She broke off the kiss and took her robe from the chair. "Hang this up when I yell, okay?" She left and closed the door. "Okay." I hung up the phone.

Post-mod is, let's face it, a yuppie outlook. It reflects an experience that takes for granted not only television, but suburbs, shopping malls, recreational (not religious or transcendent) drugs and the towering abstraction of money. To grow up post-60's is an experience of aftermath, privitization, weightlessness; everything has apparently been done. Therefore culture is a process of recycling; everything is juxtaposable to everything else because nothing matters. This generation is disabused of authority, except, perhaps, the authority of money; theirs is the bumper-sticker, "THE ONE WITH THE MOST TOYS WINS." (Perhaps the ultimate post-modern experience is to shift information bits and computer bytes around the world at will and high speed.) The culture they feel is a passive adaptation to feeling historically stranded - after the 1960's but before what? Perhaps the Bomb, the void hanging over the horizon, threatening to pulverize everything of value. So be cool. In this light, post-modernism is anticipatory shell-shock. It's as if the Bomb has already fallen.

Fratricide is only the first phase
With brother fighting brother stabbing brother
And just killing after one another
But when you see your brother blood just flow
You die fighting then you know
That the first phase must come to an end
And it's time for the second phase to show

Well where the fuck is she What about her roommate over there says Byron the one who studies philosophy she seems more your type Why do you say that She's a bit smarter and she's not married I guess those two things go hand in hand don't they Byron laughs at his own joke Stop corrupting him Raoul if he wants to get fucked he'll get fucked what's the big deal sex doesn't solve everything in fact it doesn't solve anything why don't you just leave him alone he's just a bit sick of everything Aren't we all says Frankenstein I'm just trying to help says Byron just trying to help Sweet Jane looks at me Anyway it's usually not a good idea to rely on someone else for salvation Look what happened to Frances says Frankenstein Sweet Jane smiles I have to go on pretty soon do you want me to dedicate a song to you Yeah that would be nice how about Tired of Being Alone We don't do that one any more she says.

Bad night for Sally. Emergency room duty 5:30 am a self-abortion death due to massive internal hemorrhaging the girl bled to death in her own womb. Blood everywhere the floor slick the doctor's coat soaked red on white tile red on white cotton red on white. Sally feels something awful stir in her own belly a fucking butcher knife she used a fucking butcher knife hysteria very near the surface. Sally a nurse Sally a woman Sally trying to fill out the report can't read. Black marks on white paper. No sense. Sally trying hard to comprehend trying hard to force meaning into the markings no use no sense. The markings mean nothing. Not another language no language. Language does not exist. Red on white.

Get Hooked on Aerobics!

In order for me to show you where your desire is, it is enough for me to forbid you a little.

I'm really fucking sick of this I go over to one of the large overstuffed chairs grouped around an oversize tv monitor the monitor's connected to Lautrec's camera so one can sit in the chair and look at the party nobody else is sitting here so I reach over and turn the thing off I need another drink but I don't want to get up yet Hey somebody yells to me Hey you turn that thing back on it's one of the bouncers he's walking toward me this is the very last thing I need I get up and go to the bathroom as I pass him I hear him mutter under his breath fucking asshole doesn't even know how to have fun.

Raoul has a new game. It's called Don't Read This. He walks along the streets deliberately trying not to read the street signs, advertisements, brand names, store signs, billboards, tee-shirts etc. The game is very frustrating, language is impossible to ignore. Raoul's thinking about moving to Germany because he doesn't speak german, but he realizes that that wouldn't work either, because sooner or later he'd assimilate some german, and the whole thing would start all over again. . . .

I got those 501 Blues. 501 Jeans. From Levi-Strauss.

I can not combine certain letters, as *dhcmrlchtdj*, which the divine library has not already foreseen in combination, and which in one of its languages does not encompass some terrible meaning. No one can articulate a syllable which is not full of tenderness and fear, and which is not, in one of those languages, the powerful name of some god. To speak is to fall into tautologies. This useless and wordy epistle itself already exists in one of the thirty volumes of the five shelves in one of the uncountable hexagons - and so does its refutation. (An n number of possible languages makes use of the same vocabulary; in some of them, the symbol *library* admits of the correct definition ubiquitous and everlasting system of hexagonal galleries, but *library* is *bread* or *pyramid* or anything else, and the seven words which define it possess another value. You who read me, are you sure you understand my language?)

Maybe he's right maybe I can't have a good time maybe I don't know a good time when I see it I walk around to a spot near the front door where the fuck is she I feel like I've spent my entire adult life waiting at some door suspended by indecision paralyzed by possibility I can't leave because she might show up and I can't stay because I really am sick of all this shit maybe I should wait here a few minutes then go to the bar and get another drink or maybe I should go now and then in a few minutes come back I don't know I don't move I think about Frances it hurts to breathe.

I could hear the noise of her talking outside the door but I couldn't make out any of the words. I took my pants and underwear off and then got into the bed. Now what? I gulped one of the glasses of wine, then poured another. I watched the flame from the candles for awhile. The ticking of her clock on the night table almost covered up the sound of her murmuring in the living room. I sipped the wine slowly.

What makes people think that they're morally superior to me just because I happen to wear mink? I am sick and tired of total strangers walking up to me and screaming "How many poor animals died to make you coat?" or "Murderess! Murderess!" or snottily whispering "You've got blood on your coat."

When this kiss is over
We'll start again
It will not be any different
It will be exactly the same
It's hard to imagine
That nothing at all
Could be so exciting
Could be this much fun

I want to be loved I want to be left alone did I really think that or did I read that somewhere I can't be sure I wander around for awhile getting really depressed I guess she's not going to come I go to one of the unisex bathrooms light smell of roses and ether the bathrooms are huge and immaculate this bar is famous for its johns there's a ton of people here all listening to the music and watching the party through the monitors they have installed in the stalls it seems pretty ridiculous but kind of fun at the same time there's a certain camaraderie here someone offers me a beer and a joint the camera pans over to the band who has just finished a song I see Sweet Jane standing in front of the microphone This next song is dedicated to a friend of ours who's feeling a bit low tonight I hope this makes things a little bit better I smile that was sweet even though nothing has really changed maybe things will turn out okay maybe they will and maybe they won't and maybe they will I hear someone call my name I turn around.

Some people like to go out dancing
And some people like us we gotta work
And even some evil mothers
They'll tell you life is just made out of dirt
And women never really faint
And villians always blink their eyes
And children are the only ones who blush
And life is just to die
But anyone who ever had a heart
Wouldn't turn around and break it
And anyone who ever played a part
Wouldn't turn araound and hate it
Sweet Jane
Sweet Jane
Sweet Jane
Sweet Jane

Woman is 704th

An unidentified woman yesterday became the 704th known suicide from the Golden Gate Bridge.

The woman, about thirty, jumped to her death from the east side of the span near the north tower at 2:25 p.m. A bridge worker saw her leap.

The rare force of this text is that you cannot catch it (and therefore limit it) saying: this is that, or, what amounts to the same thing, this has a relation of apophartic, of apocalyptic unveiling, a determinable semiotic or rhetorical relation with that, this is the subject, this is not the subject, this is the same, this is the other, this text here, this corpus here. There is always the question of yes, something else.